Edited by Douglas Glover & Maggie Helwig

COMING ATTRACTIONS
92

Acknowledgements: "Shiners" and "The Chmarnyk" by Caroline Adderson were first published in *Saturday Night*. "Being Mary" by Marina Endicott was originally published in *Grain* and "Orphan Boy" by Marina Endicott first appeared in *Frictions*.

ISBN 0 88750 889 8 (hardcover)
ISBN 0 88750 890 1 (softcover)

Cover art by Egon Schiele
Book design by Michael Macklem

Printed in Canada

PUBLISHED IN CANADA BY OBERON PRESS

The stories in this year's *Coming Attractions* range from Alberta to China, from the turn of the century to the present day, united perhaps by few common threads except the talent of the three young women we have chosen. Though there are no stories that are very formally experimental, the narrative structures are used to create a wide range of effects.

Caroline Adderson's work is the most varied in setting and subject. The darker side of the child's world is explored in "Shiners," while "The Chmarnyk" looks at the experience of Ukrainian immigrants in Alberta in the nineteen-twenties. Adderson lives in Vancouver and has written radio dramas for the CBC.

Marilyn Eisenstat is the most visible prose stylist of the three. Now living in Toronto, she spent many years in China and two of her stories are set there; one exploring the country from the perspective of a Western immigrant, one from within the experience of a middle-aged Chinese woman struggling in the restrictions of her society. Eisenstat's stories are brief and tense, fighting through pain to a resolution that has only a suggestion of hope.

Marina Endicott, a young writer from Saskatchewan, is markedly different. Her stories, taken from a more extensive series, deal with the lives of a girl growing up in Nova Scotia, her sister and the people around them. They are funny and touching; not free of tragedy, but shaped by the child's detachment from the troubles of the adult world, and her passionate involvement in her own crises.

MAGGIE HELWIG

CAROLINE ADDERSON

Shiners

Laurence is wading stiff-legged into the lake, plastic bucket in one hand, the other reassuring the top of his head. Their grandmother has got him to put on a little sailor cap. Blue trunks, Thad's of two years before, sag at the crotch. On his chest are raw pink marks, a tender mottling where scabs were peeled off too soon.

Sun-warmed shallows show minnows. Like the blades of small new knives, they are painfully silver, alluring. A cluster hovers over grey-green pebbles. The water is knee-deep to Thad, thigh-deep to Laurence.

Thad says, "Give me the bucket." Poised, he bends low, careful that his shadow does not cross the fish and disperse them or, blocking light, unsilver them so they disappear. He is feeling for the best moment to strike. Then Laurence sucks in his breath. Thad starts and his movement disturbs the water, sends out ripples that counter the waves and make a tiny liquid jarring. The minnows flick across the rocks, the yellow sand bottom of the lake, and away.

"Little shit," Thad hisses.

"I didn't do anything!" says Laurence.

"You breathed!"

Laurence pulls the sailor cap over his eyes. He groans. Throwing down the pail, Thad leaves the water to lie on the sand. Laurence comes and stands over him. "I didn't do anything. Thad? Or are you just mad again because you failed?"

This question is without malice, Thad knows, but it's of little consolation. He opens one terrible eye, and Laurence cowers. Even before Thad moves, Laurence begins running down the beach, arms flailing. This is why he runs so slowly, Thad thinks. Not because he has a plastic thing in his heart, but because his arms move faster than his legs and through so much air, so inefficiently. Thad lets him go a distance, then

8

leaps, sprints, catches Laurence by the swimming trunks, yanks him to the ground, pushes his face in the sand, grinds it there. Laurence sits up spitting sand out of his mouth. There is a circle of red around one nostril.

"You big shit." He tilts back his head and pinches his nose. He never cries.

Thad says nothing. He begins, though, chewing on his bottom lip, the way he does when he is sorry. When he has been unkind. He has failed at school, failed Grade 6 because he watches too much television someone said. Probably the teacher. What he misses most are the Saturday morning cartoons.

Their grandmother calls from the cabin. Thad helps Laurence to his feet, replaces the cap and walks with his arm around his brother.

She is watching the boys, the little one scurrying like a distressed insect, Thad so big and hale. She doesn't much like children, yet these grandchildren keep coming around. Thad is okay; she has a soft spot for the bad ones who can never get it right. Laurence, sick in the heart from birth, is treated too much like a holy thing, and she can't believe it hasn't gone to his head. The girls, though, are the worst with their plastic radios, flip-flop sandals and flowery beach towels, always hysterical over spiders.

She was never interested in children, yet her whole life has been kissing bloodied knees, reciting idiot rhymes, giving care. It's perfunctory second nature now. She was only thirteen, plucked from school to mother her sisters. She remembers herself in bare feet and a hand-me-down cardigan, they were that poor. The three little girls playing with a feather boa that came off a relief train. At seventeen she was working as a domestic for an engineer and his wife. She used to bring their children around to Nathan's flat and leave them with a Ukrainian downstairs who could play the accordion. While she and Nathan made love on his sofa, they heard through the floorboards the wheezing of Old World melodies, and the accordion became for them, half in jest, the most erotic of instruments. She didn't worry about the children finking because one was retarded and the other she could pinch and slap into submission and, anyway, the engineer was in love and wouldn't say boo to her.

Then looking after her own child, living with her mother and sister, suffering their self-righteousness. Nathan was in the army stationed abroad, so she wore her mother's wedding-ring. Dependency, constant petty bickering, it was the worst time for her, and as a consequence she could never love her first child. Undernourished and colicky, he repelled her. Now he's almost 50, and he wrote her a letter telling of breakdowns and divorces, saying he is unable to feel loved in his relationships, asking once and for all what she had against him. She felt sorry for him and wrote back that he was her precious treasure, when in reality he is the personification of all her woes and frustrations. She had five more children by Nathan and now has eight grandchildren.

The cabin is just beyond the beach and a narrow spread of wild grass, sitting in the shadow of pines. Crossing the grass, both boys are watchful for snakes. They are hopeful snakecatchers. Sometimes Thad turns over the stones on the path for this purpose, aggravating their grandmother because he never replaces them. They talk of pythons and boa constrictors, anacondas, but will gladly settle for less.

Carlyle, their Labrador gone blind, lies in the doorway. Thad gives one of the ears, worn and tatty as an old flag, a sharp tug. Grunting, the dog swings its head frantically, staring out of silvering eyes.

"Are you teasing again?" She stands on the other side of the screen door, a thick-middled figure in a cotton dress, white braid hanging over her shoulder. There is a cragginess in her voice that could be anger, but is really age and fatigue.

"You saw me, didn't you!"

"Shhh." She makes the sound of dry leaves on concrete, of light rain, to let him know she was not accusing. He is so sensitive. She smiles. She still has her own teeth, scary teeth Laurence says, one broken off diagonally. Shaking her head, she opens the door, handing them their T-shirts as they file past.

Although the summer days draw out, long as a skein of bargain twine, light until eleven o'clock, the cabin, in the enclave of tall pine, the circle of continual scent and shadow, is always dark. There are electric lights, but because they attract insects—great clumsy bat-winged moths, mosquitoes—their grandmother rarely uses them. Instead they have oil lamps; the boys like these better anyway.

Laurence and Thad sit opposite one another at the table. She sets before each of them an enamel dish of beans, a wiener sliced across the top. There is a story about these metal dishes, that they were given to their grandmother after their grandfather's stroke when she hurled her every piece of china against the side of the cabin. It is a story Laurence does not believe; Thad fancies she threw them at their grandfather, and that is why he had a stroke.

Thad grimaces at the food. She laughs and feels Laurences's forehead, asks, "Good day?"

"Good day!" says Laurence, full of beans.

When she goes for the lamp, Thad bends back his spoon and catapults a piece of wiener at his brother.

"We're going to get eggs after supper," she says, putting the lamp on the table. She touches a match to the wick. The flame springs, shadows slip into the room and flatten themselves around the walls.

"Do I have to go?" asks Thad. There is a girl Thad's age at the farm where they buy eggs. She wears her hair cropped and a halter top through which he can detect two soft cones of flesh. Last week she called him a lunkhead. "I won't go."

After supper they step behind the Chinese screen that separates their sleeping area from the kitchen and pull jeans over their now-dry swimming trunks. Their grandmother is in the bedroom setting up the tray for their grandfather. This visit the boys have seldom looked in on their grandfather. Not a pretty sight like he used to be, their grandmother says. The boys go out and sit on the beach and wait for her.

"What are you thinking about?" asks Laurence.

"Underdog and Bullwinkle." He traces a snakey mark in the sand with his foot, then points over the water. "Look. Do you see it?"

"What?"

"There. A canoe."

Laurence stands and, shading his eyes, studies the imaginary line where water wets sky.

"Are you blind?" says Thad.

"There isn't any canoe!" Laurence cries.

She feeds him less than gently, spoon scraping across naked gums. When she met him he was lathing broom handles in a factory, and his forearms and wrists were so large he could not close the cuffs on his shirt. That was 1935, and no other man has interested her since. Such a beautiful skull and hair she could grab in both hands and still not catch half of. Even in old age, before his stroke, she never lost physical desire for him.

When his job closed and he went on relief, she would give him her liquor rations and bring fruit and chocolate from the engineer's house. Then the war broke out and they were separated for two terrible years while she, knowing he would not be faithful, prayed that at least he would not marry overseas. He did return, but because he had run away from the army, they came up north just like fugitives and nearly starved the first winter, she pregnant again. Nathan began running fishing expeditions on the lake, and they built two cabins. One day he had a vacationing police constable as a client.

The years Nathan spent in prison, she worked in a garment factory to support their three children. When he was released in 1950, they were finally able to marry. They spent their

honeymoon night back in their cabin quarrelling through the
tense climax of realized dreams. He hit her in the face, breaking her tooth. It did not dim her happiness; such struggle was
part of love. She was always proud of his strong body and his
force, his good looks.

She wipes the flaccid face with the bib, then feels around
under the quilt, checking padded pants for moisture.

In the station-wagon, Thad climbs over the seat to the very
back and lies beside the spare tire among the clutter of egg
trays and flowerpots and old newspapers. Laurence sits in
front with their grandmother.

"We're going to have a storm," she says. "Look at that sky."

Thad presses his face against the glass and sees the thickening grey. The tree stands they pass are completely still. He
almost expects to hear Laurence suck in his breath from the
tension. When they pull into the farm, it appears deserted, the
animals gone away to wait out the rain.

Their grandmother takes an egg tray from the back as the
brothers clamber out of the car, slamming doors. She gives it
to Thad, and he and Laurence go to fetch the eggs while she
rings at the house.

The egg shed is for washing and storing. It stinks of chicken
dirt and mouldy feed. They enter, Laurence plugging his nose,
and the girl is standing with her back to them, bending over
the sink. She wears denim cut-offs and that halter-top, the
frayed ties double-knotted against boys. Her sneakers and
bare legs are muddied.

"Heggs please," says Laurence, still plugging his nose.

She turns and looks at him, her expression softly curious,
and Thad realizes she knows something about them. She sees
him.

"Lunkhead."

He reddens, but cannot think of a suitable reply.

"If you want heggs, you can wash them yourself," she tells
Laurence, feigning contempt and holding out the brush. He

grins. Last week she let him wash too.

Laurence talks to the girl as he cleans the eggs under the dribble of tap water. Thad stands behind with the tray and she loads.

"We almost caught these shiners today." He hesitates. "Thad almost caught them."

"What's a shiner?"

"A small fish. A——"

"Punch in the eye," says Thad.

She glances at him. She has blue eyes and in the left one, under the pupil, a spot of yellow. Seeing it, he immediately lowers his gaze to the bib of her halter top.

"Then I sneezed or something. Anyway, we didn't catch them after all."

"Too bad."

"Yeah. Thad got mad."

"Lunkhead," she says.

Thad reddens again. Then it occurs to him she just might know he has failed a grade. He drops the tray and shouts at Laurence.

"Why don't you shut up? Why don't you go straight to hell?"

There is a long silence. He has never said go to hell in his life. It is something he heard on television.

The girl will not look at him. She pats Laurence on the head. "It's okay. You two clean that up and I'll wash the eggs."

At Thad's feet, the yolks are the same colour as that spot in her eye.

In no time they are walking silently up to the house, Thad biting hard into his lip. She puts the tray on the hood of the car, and they go to sit on the steps. Their grandmother is standing in the parlour with the woman who owns the farm. She is a widow and the mother of the girl, Thad remembers. He can hear them now through the screendoor, talking about Laurence.

"Born that way," their grandmother says. "This year he had

an operation."

"And now?"

"He's fine, thanks be to God. They put a rubber ball or garden hose or some such thing in his heart. Be right as rain soon. Now it's the elder boy we worry about. Thad was shaken up bad."

"Because of his brother being sick?"

"You know how children blame themselves. Anyway, he had trouble at school and whatnot. Bad imaginings."

The other woman clicks her tongue softly. "He thought he was going to lose his brother."

"Oh, the temper! I see it like this," says their grandmother. "Love on account of fear is a difficult thing to manage. It wells up and gets kind of desperate. Don't we know about that? Watching husbands go?"

On the step, Laurence promises a snake. "But don't blame me!"

"For what?"

"If it steals an egg and swallows it whole!"

Driving back, all of them in the front seat, it begins to rain. Only one windshield wiper works so the brothers watch the road through blear and smear. Presently the horizon lights up in sheets, then fades, lights again, this time cut through by brilliant jags.

The worst thing about a storm is that they must stay inside. Laurence, used to long hours of solitude, hunches over the table reading a *Scamp* comic. Their grandmother washes dishes. Thad does not usually read, so he paces. Every time he passes Carlyle lying behind the telephone stand, the dog growls.

"Old shit," says Thad and he slips into the bedroom and stands staring at his grandfather.

The old man sits in a wing-backed armchair beside the bed. A patchwork quilt is tucked around his legs, his obvious knees like the bulbs of those glass telephone-wire insulators on the shelf above the sink. Though the body is aged, the face, perhaps from swelling, seems young and unlined. His eyes are a clear grey, milky hair a fringe around his glowing head. His mouth hangs slack, and a line of spittle crosses his chin, darkens his breast. Laurence is there now standing next to Thad.

On the table by their grandfather is a bowl of mints, clear like ice. Thad crosses the room and takes a candy, unwraps and pops it in his mouth, sits on the bed. He throws one to Laurence who misses and must feel around for it under the bureau.

Thad cocks his ear toward their grandfather. "What? Speak up! You want one too, Grandpa?" He grins at Laurence.

Laurence comes and takes a candy, stands there holding it, staring at the floor. Thad giggles.

"What?" asks Laurence, smiling. "What's so funny?"

Soon they are both on the bed, holding their bellies, directing their laughter into the bedspread. Neither can identify the source of this mirth; it is just one of those moments between brothers. Then Laurence sits up and puts the wrapped candy in their grandfather's mouth. Immediately he begins sucking, an innocent look of surprise on his face like an infant not expecting the nipple. The tail of cellophane between his lips turns around and around.

"Do it again!" says Thad.

It is too funny, the way the old man puckers his lips like a fish, how he tongues a second candy, gentle greed. Even when he coughs, the wrappers tickling, the brothers are stifling each other's laughter with their clowning hands.

They hear the telephone ring and tear out of the room.

"Yes, they're fine," says their grandmother. "Here they are now. Here's Laurie."

He grabs the receiver and begins babbling. "Shiners! Don't you know what shiners are? Mom! They're minnows! You really didn't know?"

Thad takes the phone and she asks him how he is doing without a television. He says he has not even noticed.

After they hang up, their grandmother herds them into the

kitchen for washing, then lets them pee from the door stoop. There is a bathroom, but that is not as much fun. She takes an oil lamp and sets it on the table behind the Chinese screen so the boys can chat before going to sleep. She lays her hand across Laurence's forehead, then kisses them both. Coming through the wall so faintly is the sound of their grandfather coughing. They strip off their jeans and T-shirts and pile onto the bed, still in trunks.

"I want that side," says Laurence, meaning the side next to the table so he'll be the one to put out the lamp.

"No way," says Thad.

"Big shit," says Laurence feebly.

Thad cuffs him on the head. "Little shit."

In the bedroom their grandfather coughs raggedly, persistently. They hear their grandmother's voice too, softly first, then rising to alarm.

Suddenly the overhead light is on. The boys have not seen electric light for almost two weeks, and it pains and startles. She is standing over them, her hair loose and her dress half-unbuttoned. They have never known her angry, and this is fury. She shakes a clotted scrap of cellophane in Thad's face.

"He was choking!"

"Laurie did it!" Thad blurts, then takes his bottom lip between his teeth.

Laurence stares animal-faced.

"Did you?"

"Yes."

Leaning over Thad, she grabs Laurence by the arm. She shakes him out wildly, like his badness is dust.

"My man, big man," she sighs, drawing his limp arm out of the sleeve, running her hands over the angles of his bones. She is naked herself, gnarly bare toes on the cold wood floor, breasts sloping to rest on the shelf of her belly. She leans into him, ear-to-ear, slides her hands under his buttocks and this way can lift him from chair to bed. The plastic undersheet crackles like fire as she lays him out long. He is staring loose-mouthed at the ceiling. She climbs into bed and lowers herself carefully on top of him, spreads her big thighs around the bracket of his jutting hips, rests her elbows by his shoulders and bends to kiss his face, his unresisting mouth. "Big man." There is no tuneful respiration of an accordion, just the rain outside rushing against the roof in wind-sent waves and the chimes that hang in the pine boughs like cymbals.

The boys lie in shocked silence staring at the ceiling beams, the hillscape shadow of their profiles on the cabin wall. Somehow a moth has made its haphazard way into the cabin and it drives itself stupidly against the lamp. Thudding, thudding. In the bedroom, their grandmother is murmuring.

Laurence sits up and, clutching fearfully at his own legs, begins to cry. Not aloud, that is not his way, though nor is crying. He just sits there staring, his face twisted, tears and mucus flowing.

"I did a mean thing!"

"Shut up," whispers Thad. He gnaws his lip.

"I did such a mean thing to Grandpa!"

"Shut up please!"

Laurence, face in hands, falls into the pillows. Spasming with grief, he clenches and unclenches his body. It seems like hours Thad must suffer Laurence's quivering, hear his cloggy, gasping breath until it finally rises to a snore twice the size of him. Then Thad is alone in the discordant night—wind chimes clashing, their grandmother murmuring, the moth's monotonous self-battering. He touches his finger to his lip and stares at it. He is bleeding.

The Chmarnyk

In 1906, after scorching the Dakota sky, an asteroid fell to earth and struck and killed a dog. Only a mutt, but Baba said, "Omen." It was her dog. They crossed the border into safety, into Canada. But the next spring was strange in Manitoba, alternating spells of heat and cold. One bright day Mama went to town, stood before a shop window admiring yard goods, swaddled infant in her arms. From the eaves above a long glimmering icicle gave up its hold, dropped like a shining spear. The baby was impaled.

These misfortunes occured before I was born. I learned them from tongues, in awe, as warnings. My brother Teo said, "Every great change is wrought in the sky."

Grieving, they fled Manitoba, just another cursed place. Open waggon, mattresses baled, copper pots clanking. Around the neck of the wall-eyed horse two things: cardboard picture of the Sacred Heart; cotton strip torn from Baba's knickers. Every morning as she knotted the cloth, she whispered in the twitching ear, "As drawers cover buttocks, cover those evil eyes!" Thus protected, that old horse carried them right across Saskatchewan. In Alberta it fell down dead.

So they had to put voice to what they had feared all along: the land wasn't cursed, they were. More exactly, Papa. A reasonable man most of the time, he had these spells. Ups and downs. Up, he could throw off his clothes and tread a circular path around the house knee-deep through snow. Or he would claim to be speaking English when, in fact, he was speaking in tongues. "English, the language of Angels!" but no-one understood him. Down, he lay on the hearth, deathly mute, Baba spoon-feeding him, Teo and Mama saying the rosary. I was just a baby when he died.

But this is a story about Teo, dead so many years. I remember him stocky and energetic, his streaky blond hair. If they had stayed in Galicia, he would have been a *chmarnyk*, a rainman. In the Bible, Pharaoh had a dream that seven gaunt cows came out of the river to feed on cat-tails. He dreamed of seven ears of corn on a single stalk, withered and blighted by East wind. But Teo never relied on the auguries of sleep. He could read the sky.

"Rain on Easter Day and the whole summer is wet. If you see stars in the morning from one to three, the price of wheat rises."

He told me this in a field still bound by old snow. He had stood out there the whole night and I was calling him to Easter Mass, 1929. "What'll it be this year then, smartie?"

"Drought." He pronounced the word like he was already thirsty. "Little sister, listen. The sky is only as high as the horizon is far."

"Well, la-di-da."

Teo was nineteen, I twelve, and the skin of my own dry lips cracked as I echoed: "Drought." All that spring, smoke rose straight out of chimneys and every evening the sky flared. "That's dust in the air already. That's dry weather," he said.

Always reading, he got an idea about the cat-tail. "Ten times more edible tubers per acre than a crop of potatoes."

"Just before a storm," he said, "you can see the farthest."

Since the price of wheat was not going to rise, Teo sold our farm and bought the store in town. There I learned our other names: "bohunk" and "garlic-eater." People didn't like owing us money, but the fact that they did never stopped them writing in the newspaper that we couldn't be loyal subjects of the British Empire. That we would never learn to put saucers under our cups. I refused to wear my embroidered blouses and sometimes even turned to the wall the cardboard picture of the Sacred Heart. It embarrassed me the way Our Saviour bared his sweet breast, as if he didn't care what people thought of him.

Teo was unperturbed. There was work to be done and I could be his little helper. At Mud Lake, by then half-receded, ringed by white alkali scum, he asked me to remove my clothes. Covering my breasts with spread-open hands, I waded in, then clung to a snag slippery with algae while Teo, on shore, named clouds.

"Cumulus. Cumulus. Cumulus."

"Why me?" I shouted.

"Needs a virgin," he called. "A smooth thigh."

I came out festooned with leeches—arms, legs, shoulder even. He chose the halest one and burned the rest off with his cigarette. All the way home I wore that guzzling leech sheltered in a wet handkerchief. Like a doting mother I nursed it. Then we put it in a Mason jar with water and a little stick.

"Leech barometer," Teo said. "Fair weather when the leech stays in the water. Unless the leech is dead."

The next year Mud Lake had disappeared. Rising out of what once was water—a secret charnel-house. Old glowing buffalo bones.

Already farms were being seized. Some families had been paying us in chits since 1929. To one farmer Teo made a gift— an idea expressed to hide the giving. "If he wanted, a man might collect and sell those bones as fertilizer." We saw the farmer working every day. On first sight of the bones his horse had spooked. Now it had to be blindfolded—led like a reluctant bride through the sweltering town, an antimacassar the veil on its head. It strained with the cart, load white and rattling. Vertebrae fell in puffs of dust on the road, provoking feud amongst the bored and forsaken dogs.

I never knew there could be so much death in one place or that the labour of removing it could be so gruelling. Finally, all the bones were in a dry heap at the train station, ready to be loaded. Women could go down and have their photograph taken with a huge skull in their lap. Boys swung at each other with the leg bones.

Strangest railway robbery anybody had ever heard of. Overnight it all vanished. Not even a tooth left on the platform. The exhausted farmer lost his remuneration. After that he posted himself in front of the store warning those who entered that Teo was not as stupid as he looked. Declaring revenge was a man's right when he thirsted for justice. He spat so often on our window I made a routine of cleaning it off. The pattern of saliva on the dusty glass was like cloudburst.

It was so dry in the Palliser Triangle, dunes of dust stopped the trains. We tucked rags around doors and window-sills, blew black when we blew into our handkerchiefs. In Galicia, Teo would have been a *chmarnyk*, a rainman. He took me with him, driving where roads were passable, farm to farm. Waiting in the car, I watched him point at the sky. Children circled, staring in at me. They thumbed their noses and wrote "garlic" in the dust on the windscreen. I kept my gaze on Teo as he exhorted skeletal-faced farmers to send their wives and daughters into the fields. Send them into the fields on Sunday morning and have them urinate, for a woman's urine has power to cause rain.

Brandishing brooms, they drove him off their porches. They kicked him in the seat of his pants.

"Why are we doing this?" I cried. His every good deed bred animosity.

Teo said, "They didn't know Our Saviour either." To give me faith, he made a drop of water appear at the end of his nose, glistening like a glass rosary bead. "That's without even trying," he said.

Nobody went into the fields, of course. Just Mama and Baba. And me, squatting, skirts hoisted. I saw my urine pool in the dust, ground too parched to drink. High in a tree a crow was watching me. It shouted down that rain comes at a cost, and even then might not come for good.

In the Bible, Pharoah dreamed of seven gaunt cows. By 1932, I must have seen 700 so much worse than gaunt. Angular with starvation or dead and bloated, legs straight up in the air.

"Ten times more edible tubers per acre in a crop of cat-tails than a crop of potatoes!"

"Who told you that?"

"And the fluff! That's good insulation! Mattress stuffing, quilt batting! From the stalks, wallboard and paper! The leaves—baskets, clothing!"

I laughed. Who would wear a cat-tail? "How come nobody ever thought of this before, smartie?"

"Lots nobody ever thought of! Every great change is wrought in the sky! God made the cat-tail!" His tongue raced, arms circled in the air.

But the big idea was cheap cattle feed, deliverance from famine. Teo the Deliverer. "Is a cow going to eat a cat-tail root?" I wanted to know.

"Cows eating pieces off tractors! Cows eating gate latches!" Hardware disease.

And the next morning he drove away from the Palliser Triangle, northward, looking for a cat-tail slough. I waited. Baba sucked on her bare gums all day, as if that way she could wet her throat. Mama—always the same stories. "Dakota. 1906. A good doggie." She raised one fist in the air, swept it down with a loud smack into her outstretched palm. Weeping, she mimed the baby in her arms. That lance of ice, it dropped right out of heaven.

Then this, another sorrow: how Papa died. As a child I thought he'd been plucked from the plough and raptured straight on high. Mama used to tell how she had clutched his ankle and dangled in mid-air trying to hold him back. Nothing could be further from the truth. He threw himself on a pitchfork. So much blood, it was like when they killed a pig. This she confessed in the back room of the store as I sat on a lard pail. Suicide triples a curse.

On the red background I appliquéd a cat-tail. The words: THE EVERYTHING PLANT. For batting I planned to use the brown and gold pollen of the cat-tail flower. We were going to string it across the back of the car when we, brother and sister, did our tour of the drought towns, made our presentation at the feed stores. We were going to sleep under it at night. I was Teo's little helper.

In the corner of every eye, a plug of dust. I was afraid of crying, of someone licking the water off my face.

I urinated again in a field.

There were no clouds to name.

Now they said we were worse than Jews, almost as bad as Chinamen. I had never seen either. On the counter they scattered handfuls of raisins, railing, "Stones! Stones!" as if they actually paid us. What could we do about fly-infested flour, rancid bacon, the desiccated mouse in the sugar? When the cash register opened, chits flew out like a hundred moths. On all these accusing faces the dirty lines were a map of the roads Teo had gone away on.

Now we wanted Teo to take us away. Baba said she could smell hatred. It smelled like gunpowder.

In Galicia, Mama said, Drought is a beautiful woman. She persuades a young peasant to carry her on his back. Wherever he goes crops wither and die, ponds evaporate, birds, songs stuck in their throats, drop out of trees. Horrified, he struggles to loosen the cinch of her legs round his waist, her grappling hands at his neck. In the end, to be rid of his burden, he leaps from a bridge. Drought dries up the river instantly and, crashing on the rocks below, our young peasant breaks open his head.

Finally, a package. Inside, a big tuberous finger, hairy and gnarled. We marvelled it was still wet.

"What is it?" Mama asked.

"A cat-tail root."

When Baba touched it, she started to cry. What did it mean? Would Teo come for us? Alive, it was holding the rain. That night, to keep it moist, I brought it to bed and put it inside me.

24

To cure fever, drink whisky with ground garlic. Eat bread wrapped in cobwebs. But I did not think it was fever. Overnight my hair had curled like vetch tendrils and my head throbbed where a horse had kicked me seven years before. Beside my bed, the leech barometer. So many years in the jar, I had thought the leech was dead. Now it shimmied out of the water and halfway up the stick.

Mama said, looking over the town, "Smoke from all these chimneys curling down." When I would not take the bread and whisky, she pulled my hair.

Just before a storm, you can see the farthest. We saw you coming miles away. Dust-maker, you were weaving all over the road, horn pressed. By the time we got Baba down the stairs and into the street, a crowd had gathered round the car. You were standing on the hood, almost naked, wet skirt of cat-tail leaves pasted to your thighs.

Mama gasped, "Teo has his father's curse."

The sere voice of a crow: *Rain costs.*

And I was partly to blame. I had given my innocence to a cat-tail root while you held its power.

From the beating part of your chest, your brow, water had begun to trickle, ribbonning downward, the sheen of moisture all across you. Motionless, arms open, fingers spread and dripping—you were sowing rain. We were sweating too, the day dry and searing, but soon you were dissolving, hair saturated, nostrils and eyes streaming culverts. Then you turned, spun round and spattered the silent crowd. Turned again, kept spinning, faster. Whirling, whirling on the slippery hood, you drenched and astounded us, became a living fountain. And then, amazing! A nimbus, seven-coloured, shimmering all around you.

In Galicia, when thunder sounds, prostrate yourself to save your soul. That day thunder discharged, a firearm, reverberating. Mama and Baba dropped to the ground. A dark curtain was drawn across the Palliser Triangle. Black geyser sky.

You bowed forward and vomited a river.

The crowd fell back. They had never seen a *chmarnyk*.

After Teo made it rain, the whole town was filled with steam, water evaporating off the streets and the wet backs of the men who carried Teo's body away. Dogs staggered out of cover to drink from the temporary puddles. And in all the fields, green shoots reared, only to wither later in the reborn drought.

They carried Teo's body away and wouldn't let us see him. "Struck by lightening," they said. How could we argue? I was only fifteen and neither Mama nor Baba could speak English. The moment he was taken, we had been rolling on the ground. But I remember clearly the presence of that farmer, the one robbed of his charnel-house, his smile like lightning. The English word "shotgun" never had a place on my tongue.

Years later Teo came to Mama in a dream. In the dream he had a hole in his chest big enough to climb into, gory as the Sacred Heart. "I have seen the face of Our Saviour," he told her. "He lets me spit off the clouds."

As for me, two things at least I know. The cat-tail root holds more than water. Every great change is wrought in the sky.

Oil and Dread

A jolt. Wide-open eyes. Every day now Des wakes like this, disoriented, a man who has been moved in his sleep. A whisper, his mother's name for him, disturbs like a finger traced around his ear. Finally, Ita's rolling over in the bed delivers him, brings time and place. Her waxy face surfaces and inhales. She is swimming in sleep. Des slides out of bed and picks off of the clothes-horse his big trousers, a shirt the size of a sail. He dresses as he moves through the small rooms, leaving the house before both arms are in his jacket.

In this treeless place the wind reveals itself in the unceasing transport of clouds, the swelling of crows on the power lines to larger, more ragged forms. Reeled in again to the water, he follows a dry-stone fence that disappears where its parts have been returned to the ground. Past *Feely's*, Ita's store, the dirty windows and milkboxes and lottery tickets that make them their living. Near the beach stands an abandoned cottage. Its rotten thatch, shiny like threads of mica, sags and stops the door. Des wades thigh-deep through nettles, leans in the paneless window. Inside, all is as it was left when years ago the vanished occupant made his break with Ireland. The blankets, drawn back on the bed, are marbled now with mildew. On a table soft with dust, a tin mug from that last breakfast.

A stone falls from the fence behind him. Des starts, smashing his head on the sill, then stands rubbing the spot: where Ita claims God touched him with His Mighty Finger when Des became a Catholic to marry her and a perfect circle of bald appeared. He is bleeding.

The dog cowers by the fence, ears flat against its black head. Its eyes roll upward as in pictures of the martyred saints.

"Fuck you."

Its tongue fawns. What Des cannot stand, even in his own dog: anything like submissiveness. With his foot, he raises the muzzle up, up until he can grab it and feel the throat block with straining. When he lets go, the dog pauses on its haunches licking around its mouth, then bounds away toward the water.

A flock of crows blows in like paper ash. The frustrated beat of the ocean. Weekends, he brings his daughters here, makes them say, as he points to the blurred false-front of Ireland's own distant coast, "Mayo" and "Sligo" and for a joke, "Newfoundland." Now this shore is home to his dread. Whatever threatens him, he feels for certain from here it will come, from the water, doom or a boatload of judges.

The dog is barking. Its tail flails as it shuttles in the surf. Tug-of-war: dog and bird.

"Hey! Leave off!" Des crosses the beach to where they are battling. At his feet, the dog is jawing a live wing. The bird, black throat open in soundless rage, twists and thrashes and rocks the dog's obstinate head. It hisses at Des, panicked bravado. Des grins. With the side of his boot he kicks the dog away.

Des needs all the strength of his big hands to clutch the bird to his chest. "I-i-i-ta!" He hammers the bed with his boot. Finally she sits up, blond hair sticking to the sides of her face as she groans at the ceiling. In Des' arms the bird convulses and, loosening a wing, flaps wildly, hisses. Ita gapes. "What are you after bringing home, you fucking crazy Des!"

"Give me a hand." He goes into the kitchen and from there can hear her fall out of bed and stumble around the room. "You're an eejit, Desmond Martin. What time is it? Didn't you hear me up half the night with Old Man and his pissing and moaning? Jesus! Some of us have a funeral to go to today! You and your creeping around at all godless hours. It's a sin."

She appears in her bare feet, nightdress, a green housecoat. Cigarette between her lips, she heads to the gas range for a light.

"Ita!"

"What? Can't I have a fag?"

"Will you look what I've got in my arms!"

She faces the bird and softens. The cigarette goes in her pocket. "What happened?"

"Oil."

"Poor thing." She begins taking the dirty dishes out of the sink. "Des, you are a saint and a lover of the wee animals."

When the sink is filled with soapy water, Des, so he can take off his jacket, has Ita hold the bird. It wrenches free immediately, smashing its wings against the counter, sloshing water on Ita and the floor. It stabs at Des' eye with the lance of its beak.

"Jesus, Ita!"

"Jesus, you!" she shrieks.

He wrestles with its beating wings. The bird collides with the window, jettisons a spray of liquid shit that just misses Ita. She screams: "The devil's in it! Fuck off! Fuck off!" When at last he recaptures it, beak in his fist, wings in the vice of his huge hand, she is laughing. "A hell of a way to get up in the morning!"

She takes a brillo pad and begins scrubbing the bird. "Was there oil on the beach?"

"None."

Hers is not to question mystery. She changes the subject. "You didn't hear Old Man last night crying for his dead brother? Course not or you wouldn't have been up at the crack of day! I had to lay out all his gear in the middle of the godless night." She pauses and sniffs. "Do you think we should have brought the girls up?"

"A funeral's no place for kids."

"At Mary's age I loved a funeral." She squints at him. "You'd be happy to leave our poor babes in Letterkenny all the year, wouldn't you? You don't love your daughters."

He sees where she is leading him. Her regular accusation. The girls come home every weekend.

"You don't. Not like I do. Every day's misery without them. I mean it when I say I'd have ten more if you'd only get a job."

She drains the soapy water, refills the sink. Next, Des knows, she will remind him he is Canadian.

Under her breath: "Sure there's more work in Canada..."

The bird twists in his hands.

"This is the only thing I have to say: when Old Man dies— God forgive me for mentioning such a thing on the very day we put his brother in the ground—when he dies we're all going to Canada."

"*We are not going to Canada!*"

"Why not? Sure you've never shown any kind of love for this country!"

He scoops the bird out of the sink, trailing a watery skirt. With its head suddenly free, it screeches, snakes a long neck toward Ita.

"Jesus!" She ducks.

Des leaves her standing in chaos. The dog has been waiting outside and is eager at his heel, but he shuts it out of the shed. He kicks clear an area on the dirt floor then shifts the spasming bird under his arm, stoops to lay down a bed of old newspapers.

Back in the house, Ita leans into the mop, dragging long on her cigarette. Her housecoat is drenched.

"What do you want?" Des asks from the door. "Sausages? I'll run over to the store."

She won't look at him. "I want you out of this hairy mood."

"What mood?"

"So tight-lipped and always sneaking down to the beach. It has to do with that Canadian boy you wouldn't bring home the other night, doesn't it?"

"Will you get off that?"

"Then it's your not drinking any more. It's the Total Abstinence Society of the Sacred Heart around here. Cutting yourself off altogether isn't healthy." She glances at him, then doubles full-face. "Did you take that off the clothes-horse?"

He looks down at himself, shirt-front ruined with the molasses-stain of oil.

30

"Is that your pressed white shirt for the funeral?" She takes the mop in her hands, a weapon, and comes raging after him.

Old Man is sitting on the edge of the bed cleaning his nose with his little finger. He seems to be looking across the room where the red Christmas bulb burns continuously under the picture of the Sacred Heart. Des coughs and Old Man looks up, frowning. He wipes his finger on the front of his undershirt and crosses himself.

"We're putting my brother in the ground today," he says. "Pray for Peter Feely."

"He was a good man." As he says this it occurs to Des that he hasn't thought of his own brother in years.

"No, he wasn't. He was just too old to be bad."

"I'm going to dress you. Have you washed?"

"I don't wash."

"Don't tell Ita that."

"*You* don't tell her."

Des gets Old Man's underwear from the bureau. Slowly, Old Man raises his arms, thin, stained in patches the colour of tea. Des peels the undershirt off his trunk, over his head, then is startled to see he has left him completely naked.

"Jesus," says Old Man. He waves his wormy hands in the air. A fumbling with the fresh shirt, an attempt to guide shaking hands into armholes, but Old Man is tangled in his own underwear. To hide what shames him, he draws up the round bulbs of his knees. Finally, his flushed face appears, glaring indignantly, showing the raw gums behind his lip. Des offers his forearm. Old Man clutches it without meeting his eye, hoists himself onto bare bowed legs.

"Did Ita hammer you on the head?"

"What?"

"There's blood where your poll is bare."

Des bends and takes an ankle, pushes a horny foot through the leg-hole of the briefs. Scrotum long on the thigh, translucent and fine as waxed paper. Old Man smells of tobacco and urine.

"Has there ever been an oil slick around here?" Des asks.

"When I was a lad, there was a fellow away in the head. He wouldn't take communion. Used to do his business down by the beach, what I don't know. Knocking stones together. One day doesn't a big wave roll up and snatch him away? We all went down and waited for the body to be spat back up. And when it came... What d'you think?"

"I don't know." Des staightens and tucks the undershirt into the briefs, lowers Old Man back onto the bed.

"Guess."

"I don't know."

"Well, what are we talking about, man!"

"I don't know what *you're* talking about."

"Oil! He was blackened all over with oil. Black like his very own soul!"

"You're full of it," says Des.

They struggle into the shirt, Des' great fingers grappling with the small buttons. Then he crosses the room and lifts the kilt that Ita has left spread over the back of a chair. A grey and blue plaid, it makes Old Man look thin and white as a stick of chalk.

"Bonnet on his chest, Peter Reely will be buried in the costume of the Blue Raven Pipe Band."

He gives Old Man his arm again so he can stand and step into the kilt. "You'll look great yourself."

Old Man sniffs loudly. "I suppose Ita thinks that since I'll be decked out same as the corpse, I'll follow quick to the grave."

"She doesn't."

"You can tell her I don't intend to die."

Des laughs. With the diaper pins Ita left on the bureau, he fixes the kilt through Old Man's shirt to his underwear.

"Then again, oh Jesus, if I never die Ita'll get tired of wait-ing and go off to Canada anyway without me."

"Listen. No-one's going to Canada. All this bloody talk

about Canada."

"It'd be a terrible thing to be left behind, a whole ocean of water between us. Who in the world'd fix my tea?"

Almost a month ago Des met that boy in the pub. Ita introduced him to Des as his "wee countryman." Afterward, neither could recall his name. They knew his face though: fresh and amazed. Later Ita would describe the dimple in his chin as the place where God's mighty finger had touched him when he was in the womb.

He was touring Europe on his break from university. "At last I hit Ireland, an English-speaking country. This old guy accosts me. He yaks for hours. Finally, I tell him I can't understand a word he's saying. He's totally surprised. *You're very clear*, he says!"

"It's not *how* they talk that gets me," said Des. "It's that there's never a bloody point to what they're saying!"

The boy leaned forward and looked at Des earnestly. "Talk to me, man. I love the boring, flat sound of your voice."

When Ita left with a pint for Old Man waiting at home, they were all drunk. She whispered in Des' ear: "Bring that poor little fucking Canadian home. He can sleep on the sofa."

"Whiskey?" Des asked. He went to the bar and bought a bottle. "Sorry it's not CC."

"S'okay," said the boy. "I can get that anytime."

The publican roared for everyone to clear out, but they were only half-finished the bottle. Outside the moon shone on the backs of the men talking in the yard. Des cradled the whiskey in one arm, took the boy on the other and led him around the pub to where the mountain's silhouette was a crouching animal. A rutted road ran straight up the slope, a track for driving sheep and the turf-cutters' donkey carts.

They had climbed for a few minutes when Des started to laugh. "Ita says bring that poor little fucking Canadian home." Then he sang it: "Brr-ing that poooor little fuck-ing Can-ay-dian hooome!"

"Ita's great," said the boy. "Ita's wild."

"First time I slept with Ita... " From both sides of the track the panicked drumming of fleeing sheep. "She got...she brought out her account book from the store. Wrote: I solemnly swear...I will marry Ita Mary Feely!"

"And you had to sign!"

"That's not all! Had to swear and sign on the line I'd convert!"

The boy whistled. "She's tough all right."

"In here, man." They had come to a half-ruined shed, three stone walls, a roof of corrugated metal. They fell inside, righting themselves to a view from high above the houses, pub, Ita's store. Des unscrewed the cap and drank, passed the whiskey to the boy who could barely find his own mouth with the bottle.

"How 'bout them Blue Jays?" said Des.

They began to snicker again, Des first, the boy catching it. They were both buckled over and howling before Des could put in words the rest of his story. Finally: "I had a laugh on Ita." Heart pumping wildly, leaning into the boy, he slurred. "Ita's account book? I didn't write my name. Wrote a different name so she wouldn't have anything on me. Desmond Martin. She was howling mad, not because she knew it wasn't my name, but because she'd been calling me Martin all along, see? I said everyone called me Martin, but she wouldn't have any such fucking coarseness, people calling each other by their surnames."

"What's your name then?"

"Martin Sinclair! Desmond was the name of my dog."

Now they were in agony, hysteria. Des could not breathe. He pounded his foot on the earth floor, whiskey overturning, both scrambling to save it, then lying in silence, aching. Eventually, Des dragged himself out to urinate. The boy called after him, "Lucky your dog wasn't named Spot!"

"Still...there's more!" Des staggered up the slope so he could urinate on the metal roof of the shed. "Already married, kid on the way—" Then his voice drowned in the rush of liquid drumming.

When he crawled back into the shed, the boy hooted. "How'd you get out of it?"

"Didn't. Ita doesn't know. Church don't know. Priest was a fossil. I think he died the day after. He'd married Ita's old man, too, for Christ's sake!"

"Jesus. There's a word for that... "

"Lots of words. Fucking-against-the-law are some of them." He could see the boy's amazement. To Des it was clear what the joke had turned into: this was how much he had come to love Ita.

"She was pregnant?"

"Not Ita! Back in T.O. *Shit... Did I say that?*" Des laughed and felt around for the bottle. The boy did not reply.

"It's fourteen years dead. I was your age, for Christ's sake. I never told anyone before."

Silence. Des hoped the boy had passed out. He took another swig of whiskey, the after-taste caustic.

"Asshole," said the boy.

Des shoved him hard against the wall, then let him go. The boy struggled to his feet, groaning. He lurched forward and out of the shed while Des poured over his own head the remaining whiskey. Cold down the contours of his face, it seeped in and burned his eyes.

He thought the boy had gone out to urinate. "Oh, Canada!" A minute later: "Fucking little Can-ay-dian!" Now Des stumbled out of the hiding place, into the wide open side of the mountain, white light, cold face of the moon. The boy was gone.

Ita sets the teapot in the middle of the table. Old Man, still in his piper's costume, bonnet askew, sucks on his gums and stares straight ahead. After a long silence, he sniffs. "Aye, we buried him well."

With a long even-toned cry, Ita collapses onto the table. Her back begins to tremble and her hands open wide like fans.

Soon she is shaking the table, sobbing, the teapot lid rattling.

Old Man sneers. "Shut up, Ita. It's too late for the banshee."

She straightens, face red, smeared with tears and mascara. She forces out her jaw and her fist hammers the table with such force that Old Man quivers. "Fuck you!" Ita roars. "Who was up all night listening to your pissing and moaning? I was, you bastard!" Back of her hand over her forehead, she rolls her eyes, imitating Old Man. "Me God, me brother's dead and I'm the last of the true Blue Ravens! Me God, I never liked him and in heaven he'll know it, too! I'm afraid to die meself!"

Old Man turns red and sniffs.

"Lay off him, Ita," says Des.

"Don't you tell me what to do!" Suddenly she springs from her chair and lunges for Des, grabs a handful of hair in one hand, smacks him again and again with the other.

"I-i-i-ta!" He sinks into her breasts, trying to push her away. Old Man claps his hands, cackling. Then Ita falls forward with her arms around Des' neck, sobbing again, shuddering.

"Oh, Jesus!" she cries. "Oh, Jesus! My uncle is dead and my children are in Letterkenny!"

Both men give up a roar of laughter. Ita, tears suspended, rises on her knees. "That's funny?"

"Shhh." Des pulls her close.

"With that eejit's carrying on, I didn't get my sleep last night. I'm exhausted. I don't know what I'm doing."

"Ach," says Old Man. "If you don't know, Ita, then we're really lost."

"What's the matter with you, Des? Why won't you tell me? Don't you love me anymore?"

"More than ever."

Old Man mutters as they kiss. He clears his throat. Now that Ita is off her guard, he takes the opportunity to expectorate into his saucer.

"Des, something bad is going to happen. I feel it."

"Shhh." He kisses her again.

Old Man looks up, crossing himself alarmedly.

Des pours a cup of tea and puts it in Ita's hands. She takes her chair. For a long time they sit in silence, then Old Man begins a long recounting of the funeral events.

"I'll go and have a look at that bird then," says Des.

It is not where he left it on the newspaper. He finds it behind some paint cans, wings half-spread, head lowered. Reaching down, he wags his fingers, expecting assault. The bird does not move. It has stiffened in the corner trying to extend wide its wings where there is no space, trying to stretch out its life. The black eye is still a shiny bead. Des carries it out of the shed and throws it over the fence into his neighbour's field.

Ita is undressing in the bedroom. In a half-slip and brassière, she is hanging her black dress in the wardrobe.

"The bird's dead."

"Not another body to bury. I've had enough."

"I'm going up the mountain to see if a slick's coming in."

"You're away in the head! I thought you were going to open the store!"

He is already in the car when she appears at the front door clutching closed her blouse and waving to him. He unrolls the window.

"Leave something at the holy well for my uncle!"

Earlier that afternoon he drove in the funeral cortège, Old Man beside him, Ita in back leaning over the seat to brush her father's shoulders or straighten his baldric. Old Man stared ahead at the pipers marching on either side of the hearse. Finally, he passed comment. "That's a god-awful noise they're making." When Des turned around to look at Ita, he saw how the procession trailed, mourners in black fighting the wind.

Later at the grave site, Des was one of the men lowering the coffin into the earth. The rope did not burn or harm his hands. The coffin was as light as if they were burying Peter Feely's soul without his body. As they worked, hand-over-hand, Old Man stood at the top of the grave with the big drum. Head high, dried bloom on the long neck of a plant gone to seed, jaw set, staring fiercely.

Coffin in place, they drew the ropes out of the grave and waited in silence, mourners' feet apart to brace against the wind, priest's robes swollen and rippling. They were watching Old Man as he slowly raised the baton. He poised, a salute, mourners suspended. From a distance, the falling broken voice of a crow. When the arm dropped, the drum sounded relief—a hollow bottomless beat stronger than the wind's hoarse breathing. Then, as if in retaliation, the wind snatched Old Man's bonnet from his head and set it sailing through the tombstones.

And the power of Old Man's sacrifice for his dead brother, all his strength in a sound, rocked Des and gave him the vision of his own brother. He saw him at age thirteen or fourteen, bird-cage bare-chested, hair raised on his head and mouth torn open, a scream of indignation, some long-forgotten injustice. The first time Des had thought of his brother in years was earlier that day, dressing Old Man. He was puzzled why he remembered him yet again, in childhood now instead of as he had seen him last, in his twenties, grown to manhood. Drum sounded again. Scream persisted. Peter Feely's daughter was keening for him.

Driving through the village, Des does a double-take. A boy on a bicycle waves at him and for a second Des thinks it is the Canadian. He sees one almost every day now, these look-alike, pretend Canadians, and wonders where they have suddenly come from. Passing the pub, he continues up the mountain until he meets a herd of sheep chewing cud in the middle of the road. They do not start or move when he sounds the horn. Only when he opens the door and steps onto the road do they heave and bolt. Minutes later, the road runs out. He has driven most of the way up the mountain and will now follow on foot the ridge of its naked back.

The first part of the ascent is steep, a muddy sheep track

around broken faces of stone. The heather, past its prime, is a cover of papery blossoms faded brown and coral. His big boot misses the track, sinks into the peat and sometimes scrapes away the green skin of the mountain, exposing bare-bone rock. When he comes over the top of the first plateau, sweating and breathing heavily, the wind strikes him hard. From now on it will be twice the labour, climbing and bending into the wind.

Ocean before him, sky above it an unspoiled blue, though the land is still tamped down with cloud. He rests on a rock, folding to streamline himself in the wind. Turf-cutters have left here long strips of scarring. A nearby ram pauses to look at him, horns ingrown and curling to cage its skull. He thinks again about Ita's ironic hectoring when he turned up in the middle of the night without that Canadian lad. She woke when he was climbing into bed, asked where the boy was, then bashed him around with her pillow for his thoughtlessness. She harped for days.

The wind puts him on his feet. He climbs to the next plateau, the one before the summit, cliffs two thousand feet above the ocean. And now, staring over the grey sea, a mirror of his own foaming agitation, he hears the smash of breakers on the rocks below. The sound is like Old Man's drum. The priest's words at the funeral: every one of us shall give account of himself to God. This is what has been waking him, shivering and nauseous, all along. Why at dawn he finds himself on the beach staring back at where he came from. One way or another, in this world or the next, sooner or later, truth will out.

For fourteen years, when he has thought of his other wife, she has been lying on her back in bed, mound of pregnant belly pushing up under the covers. Fourteen years later, she is sleeping still. She has not even rolled over. The fetus, arrested in the womb, floats patiently in its liquid world. All is as he left it the morning he emptied her purse and, walking out in the sunshine, broke with Canada. The blows he inflicted, her cries. The ocean and a gull wheeling below the cliff. She never told him no. Never said, "Martin! Stop!" It made him crazy, her passivity. Meaner, his own shame. When he first came to Ireland, he saw a hag in a churchyard. He felt her, even at a distance, searching his soul. She spat at him and this was joy— to know he could be resisted and saved from himself. Then he met Ita. He has been loved better than Ita loves him, even excepting her animal ways, but he has never loved more himself. He has been employed by love.

Above the nearly vertical cliff, the air is condensing on the green peak. It clots, whitens, swells, then is released to cloud over the land. And now, having reached the secret place where clouds are born, he is reminded of another birth. The image he saw at the funeral, his brother as a child, was the image of his own son.

He turns to the ocean. For a long time he stands leaning into the wind, watching the wavering line of horizon. As he stares, his eyes dry and tire and when he finally sees what he has come to see, he cannot be sure that such straining outward has not turned his vision back into himself. Far out in the Atlantic a dark bubble appears. It vanishes easily enough, only a pin-head at this distance. When it surfaces again it is larger, swollen, a blister on the water. He does not actually see it burst. Suddenly slick and black and glittering. It is spreading, moving toward shore, mourning, a funeral cortège. The stickiness of oil and dread.

Running down the mountain, not the way he came, down a spongy slope to the holy well. At the standing stone, he stumbles. Sacred carvings worn to pocked illegibility, he must touch to read. Fingers tremble over depressions, warnings, a child's face, a country. The well itself—a tiny spring trickling into a circle of stones, all around rusted offerings. He digs in his pocket, flings all the coins he has.

MARILYN EISENSTAT

Late Winter and Spring

Li Hua Weng, Professor Emeritus of the Department of Education of Guizhou Normal University, is one of the only people visible on the campus in the baking heat of the noon hour. She picks her way through the rubble of new construction and stands outside the doorway of a makeshift bamboo hut. The hut is in a row of shelters that house the construction workers—peasants from the countryside. She shouts something, but her throat is dry and she has to move closer to shout again.

A young man, naked except for a pair of shorts, comes to the doorway. His face is crumpled with mid-day sleep, and he squints in the sudden light, seeing first the outline of a thin young girl, and then as his eyes adjust, an old woman.

Li Hua falters as her thin-soled shoes find purchase in the rocky ground.

"I'm looking for Xiao Wei, comrade," she says. Her voice, with its educated northern dialect, seems to surprise the man. From her clothing, she could be a peasant too.

"Xiao Wei's in the hospital." The man coughs and steps back into the cooler darkness of the interior.

"Did he become ill in the heat?"

"I didn't see. They told me he started to scream at the construction site. At first they thought a snake bit him. But he said it was his stomach. Or his heart. Three workers carried him to Hospital Number Nine."

Li Hua's legs are trembling. After a moment, she turns onto a main path up a hill to the campus gate and onto the street that leads to the hospital.

Li Hua's legs tremble under her as she walks over stones. The gossip flows around her like water. She, rare spinster bird, proud stubborn old she-goat, political purist, stoic beyond measure, this cold one, old hard political icon, she Li Hua Weng, has become unbalanced. By a young man, a construction worker, a peasant.

The walk to Hospital Number Nine takes close to an hour. Several times Li Hua has to stop under a tree or in a rock crevice to catch her breath or to rest from the sun. The final stretch of road is unshaded and dusty. She holds her handkerchief over her mouth and nose and counts her steps. From the Cultural Garden at the side of the road she hears a distorted rendering of a Western song. The heat is seeping through her cotton shoes.

Approaching the hospital, she passes a young man carrying someone on his back. The human weight is small, covered with a flowered quilt even in this heat. A limp hand hanging outside the quilt is that of an old person. The young man trudges along sweating from the weight, planting his feet firmly and looking straight ahead.

At the kiosk outside the hospital gate, Li Hua buys a bar of soap, a green towel patterned with bamboo and pandas, a toothbrush and toothpaste. By making a plan, Li Hua wipes away the possibility that Xiao Wei is dead. She chooses a cream-coloured enamel cup with a peony design and tells the girl to wrap it carefully. She thanks the girl, calling her "comrade." At the registration booth inside the hospital gate, she learns that Xiao Wei is in the internal medicine wing.

The ward is dark and cooler than outside. The quiet murmuring of the patients and their family members stops for a few seconds when Li Hua enters. Xiao Wei is sleeping. His hair lies in streaks on his sweaty forehead. Li Hua arranges the things she has brought on the table beside his bed and stands beside him, while several people scramble to find a wooden stool for her. She will not awaken him, perhaps he has had a sedative, so she sits on the stool waiting. Eventually the sun creeps past the bars on the window, and the room darkens. A few people discuss turning on the overhead light. Someone pulls the string, there is a sizzling sound, and the light comes on, but it is so weak that it makes little difference.

A fat woman in a stained white coat comes in with a clipboard. She assumes that Li Hua is the sick man's mother or aunt. She asks Li Hua about food, and Li Hua instructs her to bring chicken broth. The woman whines that it is more expensive, more labour. Li Hua promises to pay the woman tomorrow. She feels very tired.

"What are you doing here?" Xiao Wei's voice sounds hoarse and weak, and Li Hua is embarrassed that she has fallen asleep. As she edges back to wakefulness and as her eyes adjust to the even darker room, she realizes that his hoarseness is anger.

"I brought you things you need."

Xiao Wei motions her to come closer. "Tell your maid to send word to my village that I will go home soon. I cannot work here any more. Do not come here any more. They will laugh at you. Bring me some cool water and go."

The doctor is a tired small woman with deep circles under her eyes and a voice as deep as a man's. She tells Li Hua that Xiao Wei's appendix is tender, that they will wait a day or two before deciding whether to operate. Li Hua says she will have word sent to Xiao Wei's family who live 200 li away, that she will cover any extra medical expenses. The young man, she says, works on the campus and has done some work for her in her home. He is a distant cousin of her maid.

On the way out of the hospital, Li Hua sees the man who was carrying the human load under the quilt. He is sitting beside one of the beds that are set up in the hallway. The human load is an old woman with cheekbones like knuckles on her wasted face. Her hair is spread across the pillow like stands of white seaweed.

Xiao Wei first came to Li Hua's house early in winter to visit her maid who came from the same village. The maid asked him to fix Li Hua's stove and when he refused to take money for his work, Li Hua told her maid to prepare dinner for him. He was a quiet man, no more than 30 with doe eyes and long fingers. His hair was flecked with early grey. He spoke softly with limited words. It was Li Hua's custom to eat alone, and the soft presence of her maid and this young man reminded her, as they sat around the warm stove, of animals nesting together against winter.

Li Hua asked Xiao Wei simple questions at first—how many people were in his family, how many pigs they owned, why he had decided to leave his commune to work in construction on the campus. She enjoyed his honesty and directness. Each time he came, he repaired something in Li Hua's house. The maid prepared a dinner, and Xiao Wei would stay to watch television. If a few days passed and Xiao Wei didn't come, Li Hua would become restless, and she would comment on how many things around the house were falling apart.

While Li Hua didn't admit any changes to herself, the change in her life did not go unnoticed by her neighbours. People taking late night strolls would notice the light in Li Hua's front window burning longer in the evenings. Her maid's basket often contained fresh eel or quantities of fruit large enough for a family. The maid, benefiting from the better food and warmer rooms, knew that Xiao Wei was the source of these changes, but she kept silent, because the bird that sticks out its head is the first to be shot. And when a distant acquaintance of Li Hua questioned her neighbour Old Lu about the changes in Li Hua's household, Old Lu looked up at the smoke winding from her chimney and said, "Yes, the rice is whiter and for the first time Li Hua is allowing a man to smoke in her house."

A new curtain appeared on Li Hua's window during the Spring Festival. Some said it was outrageous, truly, a dark jungle pattern of brown with green palm trees. Tigers sat on the branches, and the moon shone through the leaves. From the lighted room at night, they said, tigers seemed to stare out directly into the darkness with a gold sheen. They wondered, was Li Hua losing her mind?

As spring came and the heavy rains let up, Li Hua knew that Xiao Wei's construction project would be over by summer, and she tried to slow the time down. When the sky darkened before evening, she would get up from her desk and walk to the doorway to smell the air and feel the breeze on her face. On cloudy days, she would wait for the first raindrops to hit the ground, and for something to lurch inside her. At night, sleepless, she listened to wind and to the small animals that wandered on the hillside outside her window. She had always heard the piercing joyful sound of her neighbour Old Lu's thrush, but now she listened just as carefully to the clean after-silence. In the same way, she listened to Xiao Wei's breath in the silence of the evenings as they sat outside in her hidden courtyard, and she watched the mime of his hands absently performing a task in his memory.

Li Hua wondered. What would it be like to have a brother, a husband, a dear friend, someone who would sit with her in her rooms always in the evening? Was it really so simple, this companionship and ordinariness that she had run from all her life?

On International Women's Day, Li Hua asked the maid to make a special dinner. The three of them ate the rich meal, and commented on the signs of spring. There was an opera on the television, and the bird-like cries of its young lovers made Li Hua restless. She said she was tired, would they mind leaving early?

Li Hua, staring at the curtains as if searching their jungle patterns, fell asleep that night in her chair. Later when she awakened, she walked out and stood on the small strip of earth outside her house. She stood there for a long time. She remembered her childhood and the voice of her education.

Eat the rice first, don't take meat until the others have filled their bowls, and when there is not enough meat, eat more rice, and if there is not enough rice, drink water. Use the tea leaves three times, the third cup is the most delicious. Sit in the lowest chair,

(The night air filtered through her sleeves.)

46

serve the people, find nobility in labour, be a candle, burn yourself out in offering light to others, train your body, deny the past, harden the heart, learn from peasants.

(Li Hua ran her fingers along her arm and hugged her shoulders, swaying back and forth, a scarecrow shadow.)

And was this the outcome? At the age of 70, with a shriveled stomach and a hoarse voice, you could no longer wait for the third cup of tea, you craved the soft meat and not the gritty rice, your body erupted in a foreign longing for something so simple, so unpolitical, a quiet man burning beside you.

Old Lu, insomniac next door, heard Li Hua's sigh, a cry that peasants make. Ah Ya, Ah Ya.

Wildly, Li Hua thought of a plan. She could adopt Xiao Wei. As her adopted son, he could live comfortably with her in this small house, and as time went by he would learn to take care of her in her infirm years. When she died, he would inherit the house and her possessions. He could find a wife then, and continue to live and work here on the campus.

One evening she turned off the television and told him her plan. In response he smoked cigarette after cigarette in silence and then, without looking at her, left her rooms.

She waited restlessly for a few days for his return, and even tried to remember a prayer that she had learned as a child, from missionaries, a prayer for the return of lost things. The weather was humid, and in her restless attempt to bring more air into the stifling room, she tore the curtain off its precarious hook. The jungle design of tigers and birds remained draped over the now inactive stove. One sweltering afternoon, she finally went to look for him and learned that he was in the hospital.

Li Hua returns to the hospital daily for the next week. Xiao Wei seems neither sick nor well. His face is pallid, and he has little energy. Sometimes she feeds him. He responds in monotones to her questions, and she, thinking that she must fill the long silences, begins to tell him about her life. This opportunity to sit quietly and talk about herself is new to Li Hua. As she sits on the small stool beside his bed and tells him about the wide streets in Nanjing, or the wheeled stalls where she could buy hot chestnuts, or the huge chestnut trees themselves and their unusual fruit, she sees ahead of her some day in the future when she herself will be older and weaker. But her mind will still be bright, and he will visit her and sit in the bamboo chair beside her bed and tell her stories. He will feel the same openness and newness of telling someone else about his life. And he will take care of her. By caring for him now, she thinks, she is teaching him the way, showing him that they need each other.

Li Hua never mentions the last conversation they had in her home, about the adoption. The panic she felt that hot afternoon when she went to look for him is forgotten. Meanwhile Xiao Wei seems stronger. The doctor says they will still have to wait and see. Li Hua knows that she is neglecting her translation work, and that she cannot keep making excuses for the delay in sending the promised articles to the Capital Press.

On National Children's day, the town is unusually crowded with shoppers. Street vendors are selling little monkeys on sticks, monkeys that twirl mischievously and do somersaults if you change the stick's position. The department stores are crowded with mothers holding cotton shirts up against the obedient bodies of small children, and the shoe vendors are doing a fine day's business. Li Hua moves through it all happily, storing details for Xiao Wei.

When she gets to the hospital, Xiao Wei's bed is empty. Her first reaction is happiness. Probably he is feeling better and has gone for a walk. Then she notices that the peony mug she brought for him is not on the table beside the bed. The room, full of the usual visitors tending the sick, is silent, and the few familiar people who usually say hello to Li Hua or fetch her a stool, seem busy, with their faces turned away. From their turned away faces and their silence, Li Hua realizes that Xiao

Wei is gone. Behind the silence, she imagines she hears laughter. Stupid old woman, not a relative, just a stupid old woman doting on a young man. They have been listening, laughing quietly, not knowing who she is, just aware that she is an old woman making a fool of herself.

By the time she finds the doctor, Li Hua's hands are shaking. The shadows under the doctor's eyes seem more leaden, her coat shabbier. Matter-of-factly, the doctor says that Xiao Wei's older brother came to the hospital yesterday afternoon. Li Hua clutches her plastic purse to keep her hands from shaking. The brother asked permission to take Xiao Wei home. The doctor looks into Li Hua's eyes and speaks and waits for her reply.

It is dark already. Although Li Hua feels no hunger in her stomach, her head feels light. When she reaches a pile of rubble that separates two paths, she doesn't stop to think which path will lead her back to the hospital's front gate and the main road into town. She chooses the path that leads closer to the river. The road is lined with people sitting on low stools outside the doorways of their small shacks, fanning themselves. Old men, bare chested in the heat, rock grandchildren on their knees and sing folksongs to them. The hot air holds the smell of urine and rotting vegetables. From a distance she hears some children's songs and the confused babbling of television sets.

When the road narrows onto a dirt path she continues to walk toward the thickening darkness, leaving the houses behind her. The air is becoming more sour. It is harder for Li Hua to breathe, and something cuts into her foot through the cotton shoe. By angling her foot a certain way, she can avoid the stinging bite of the wound when it touches the ground.

Ahead of her is a large building built on the riverbank. From its high windows, troughs stretch into the river, and from inside the building she hears squeals and something that could be mistaken for human moans. Dark water is rushing through the open troughs into the river, and suddenly she

49

knows that she is near the town's slaughterhouse. Xiao Wei told her that with the money earned from raising two extra pigs, a peasant can get around the government's restriction of one child per family, by paying the tax levied for extra children. These days, more pigs are being raised, more illegal babies are being born.

The man coming toward Li Hua is the night watchman. His hoarse shouts startle Li Hua and from somewhere inside her she hears a woman babbling. He comes alongside her and takes her shoulder into the curve of his arm. Her whole body is trembling, and soon, to help her move, he is half carrying her. He is almost as confused and frightened as she is. He doesn't know who she is and doesn't know what to do with her. She seems to be mumbling in another language. He takes her to the bamboo shelter where she can lie on the straw mat where he sometimes sleeps before daybreak. She is shivering, this old woman, and he has no tea or hot water to warm her stomach. He is afraid that she will die, and afraid to go into the building to tell the night foreman what he has done. She is as small as a child. She babbles, and then he lets her sleep.

At daybreak, when his shift ends, he does not return to the hut, out of fear. He continues along the river path that skirts the town and walks back to his village and to the fields that wait for his tending.

When the night guard returns to his post in the evening, he is afraid to approach the small hut where he left the old woman, who maybe was a devil, sleeping. And if she was human, what if she is dead?

She is not there. On the straw mat where she lay he sees a stone. When he lifts it, he finds 40 yuan, more money than he makes in a month. At first he is afraid to pocket it, but when he thinks of giving it to his son, who is saving money to buy a pig, his heart feels lighter.

The Gardens of Suzhou

"The aim of the garden is to create as many perspectives as possible within a confined space"—*Nagel's Guide to China*.

We have been here in Suzhou for several days and still have not visited the gardens. Even when we buy chocolate we talk about illusions and reality. We have been in China long enough, and as we walk through the streets we indulge each other, allowing microcosms to blossom everywhere. But still we have not visited the gardens.

Our hotel, hermetically sealed, is getting hotter and hotter. The men at the desk are polite enough to us, and answer our questions by claiming they know nothing. Then they laugh when we turn away. Nearby at the hotel bar, a young American woman has been sitting for several days, drinking beer.

Yesterday we saw some American college students at the bus stop in town. The woman was tall and clean, with stud earrings, short well-cut hair, and long legs. Her expansive waist gave her an arrogant look. When I see foreigners, new and clean like this, I feel shabby. The younger of the two men was tall and ruddy, exuding vigour. In the bus line, he reached down and placed his hand over the tiny old woman beside him. His hand lightly traced the silver edges of her hair. The friends smiled. The girl fiddled for her camera. Among the Chinese, nothing happened. The old woman stood there without turning, without moving. The people around us watched the American's movement. His hand continued its path across the old woman's hair. She stood there, without moving.

And so it is. We act. We wait for a response. And they are not moved.

(That last night in Sichuan I finally visited his room. I walked through the dark corridor where laundry hung, I heard muffled voiced behind curtained doors, someone singing softly. In his room, I sat like an obedient child, scanning the ashtray full of stubs, the frayed calendar pasted on the wall. He sat on the chair, and I sat on his bed with my legs dangling over the edge. The room was so small I could have stood in the middle and touched each wall with a fingertip. Bars on the windows, tiny keys in locks in the drawers. The bed was hard, the summer cotton blanket folded neatly across one corner, the pillow perfectly aligned on the woven mat that felt like snakeskin. He was singing a song to say goodbye to me, and I told him, don't sing, it feels like death. He smiled and continued to sing, as I listened to time passing. Then he peeled an apple with a small knife so that the skin looped around his knuckles and the apple twirled in his hand. He split the apple and scooped out the seeds and handed me half. Unmoved. Or so it seemed.)

Late one afternoon, we visit a garden. The air is cooler and the streets are mottled with shade from plane trees. In the garden, every corridor leads to a closed door. There is rubble everywhere. We wander in two circles, following the symmetry of our entrapment, and leave. At the entrance, when we paid our fee, no-one told us that the garden was closed.

We eat dinner in the huge hotel dining-room. The town of Suzhou is small enough and foreigners few enough that we have seen them all already. Beside us is an older couple. The man is large and heavy. The wife is large too, her clothes draped and faded, reminiscent of the sixties. Her hair is long and pulled back, grey like her skin. Both of them look very tired, perhaps beaten. They discuss their meal with the waiter for a long time. The waiter nods continuously. When their meal comes, they push it around their plates silently, then leave.

At night, we walk alongside the canals. People sit outside their homes on small stools, rocking their children, playing cards. Old women sit in doorways knitting or shredding small strips of cloth. The doorways behind them lead to inner court-yards framed by doors of elaborately carved wood, into rooms with brick floors and oversized pieces of carved mahogany furniture. As always the dimensions seem wrong. It is the sense of space, so different from the one we are used to, that disarms us.

These Suzhou houses are different from the crowded hovels of Sichuan. In Sichuan, when we walked at night, we passed houses of dense blood-brown mud, windowless, crowded with bamboo baskets in the doorways. The houses rested against hills that looked like swirling breasts, with crops braided along their soft contours. There the air was muggy, cat's breath mingled with sewage. We struggled there in Sichuan, against something uncoded, something not in the place but awakened by the place. We were relieved to escape the poverty, and sometimes we say we are happy to have come to Suzhou, with its artificial garden microcosms and landscapes of illusion. To say goodbye to China. And Sichuan still lingers like a film over our eyes.

We are two women, one concerned with space, and the other with time. All year Linda, concerned with space, drew maps. On scraps of paper, using delicate lines and smudged outlines of watery China inks, she would start with the orderly arrangement of our foreigners' compound. She counted the bars in the gates, the trees along the border, the alternate planting of rhododendrum and roses, the angles of the arbour and the pattern of tiles along the path to the dining-room. In mapping our route to the foreign language building where we taught, she took into account each rise and dip in the land-scape, and painted the teaching building in smudged coal-black ink.

Then, for months she abandoned landscape and tried to sketch the diagonal arrangements of muscles on the peasants' backs, engraved, it seemed, by the bamboo poles across their shoulders. Were these configurations of muscles genetically imprinted, she asked. Each week, and then as spring came, almost daily, she rearranged the furniture in her room, until finally the table stood in the centre, overflowing with the detritus of several months: postcards, wrappers, characters scrawled on scraps of paper, photographs of her family, a Christmas card, a crossword puzzle and paper flowers her students made to wrap around bare branches in the winter.

Toward spring, she returned to her maps of the campus. She taped large sheets of paper around the room and began from the edges, first tracing out the hills around the campus. Then the buildings, looking like Monopoly blocks dropped into the hillsides. Coalpiles. Carved hedges. Until we left, the map not yet finished.

We visit another garden. In the corner of a small courtyard, three slender bamboo stalks lean against each other, the feather leaves rustling against a latticed window. There is a rock garden, and fat fish in a pond. Each small window built into a wall has a different pattern of latticing, and looks onto a different framed landscape. Sunlight dapples the leaves, touches the white walls stained with rain. Time goes slowly, and stills our footsteps.

As we walked along the canal one night, we smelled garbage burning. In the distance we saw a fire on the roadside and heard wailing. As we came closer, we saw three women standing by a fire. There were white ribbons in their hair, ribbons streaming down their backs. They stood in the street, wailing, while a few meters away a family sat quietly in the courtyard outside their house. We walked past, two foreign women, seemingly unmoved.

There are moments when we awaken stunned and thickened from the humid night, like animals who have stood too long under the sun. On a morning like this, we try again to visit the most famous of Suzhou's gardens, The Garden of the Humble Administrator. It is too big. We find no place to sit and finally find a resting place looking over shrubs onto a heap of debris. Then from a small teahouse we watch the Chinese tourists walking by aimlessly. Here we are, they seem to tell us, so now what do we do? Tell us what to see. We are all children. My tea leaves float like swollen seaweed. The tea tastes of hot green slowness.

Often we discuss how to throw away our gifts. Between us we have brought from Sichuan two ceramic eagles, two owls, a horse, two deer, two white vases, a rubber doll's head and neck, a goddess ashtray, salt and pepper shakers, a cat. Shall we take them out into the street, one by one, at night, looking for trash cans? Drop them in the canal? Shall we set up our own free market outside the hotel? Before dawn, shall we walk out and line this porcelain menagerie outside the hotel door? Our own absurdity wells up in these conversations. The morning after we leave anywhere, someone sifts through our garbage.

I think about time. These days, which have stretched like an eternity, will soon snap shut. Tomorrow we travel to Shanghai, from where Linda will leave for New York and I, a few days later, for Vancouver. I watch as she prepares clothing for the trip, all black except for a tin pin that a friend in Sichuan gave her. In Shanghai we will become public property again, smiling frayed foreigners with strange habits. Someone will meet us, arrange our hotel, officiously demand that we be ready for our taxi three hours early. As they shake our hands and wish us well, they will be sure to take our identification papers back. Linda will walk up the staircase in the middle of the huge reception area at the airport. She will turn back to smile slightly, shrug a shoulder and hitch the knapsack higher on her back.

It is our last afternoon in Suzhou. This is Suzhou's smallest garden, The Garden of the Master of the Fishing Nets. The gardens are not ours. We pass through and borrow their spaces, their absence of colour that invites us to see shape. Since our time will soon snap shut, I think of them at other times, under snow, at nightfall, the corridors in rain, wine cups bobbing in the stream in afternoon sunlight of another dynasty, an old man in a silk coat, The Master of the Fishing Nets, at dawn, surveying the world he has created. China. The Middle Kingdom. The Place Under Heaven. We have been here only for a moment, and have hardly understood anything.

We are sitting on a stone bench in the garden's square courtyard, under an arbour formed by the gnarled intertwining of narrow branches. Three teenage girls pass by, holding their bodies awkwardly in their straight skirts and high-heeled sandals. They are eating ice-cream bars and chatting. It is late afternoon, and cooler now. As I walk out, I look at the map of the garden, carved into one of the outside walls, hardly recognizing where I have been.

Still Born

Okay. Focus and breathe. I am a woman wearing a yellow sweatsuit on a Sunday morning, getting out of my car, picking my way through an unfinished construction of flagstone and wooden beams rising to the porch of my sister Karen's house. Five balloons on strings are slapping against the roof of the porch—a yellow one, a blue one, and three pink ones. Over the door is an unevenly printed sign, "Happy Birthday, Sara!!!!!"

Use the key to get into the house, sneak in, go right to the kitchen. By all means don't think about how the kids will stare, what they will say.

My sister Karen's arms are outstretched, and I move willingly into them. She kisses me with something sugary still on her lip. Through the mass of her hair crowding my cheek I say, "I can still do things, you know. I'll get to the kids later. I'd prefer kitchen duty first."

Karen holds me for a second longer, then pulls back, businesslike. "The sandwiches need cutting. They're in labelled plastic bags in the fridge. Gloria made them yesterday before she left. The kids are supposed to be here at noon, but they'll be late. You know—Sunday school, grandmothers, skating lessons... " Her voice trails, hesitates, then brightens. "The Sunday yuppie rush hour. I invited the whole class. Boys, too."

As she speaks, my mind divides into love for her soft benevolence and that other feeling that drags me away into private despair, a dog gnawing on the bone of other people's family life.

I clear away a spot on the kichen counter in front of the window and start to cut the sandwiches. There are enough for me to get a rhythm going: take three out of the bag, line them up, then with a kitchen knife I trace an X through them and line up the quarters on plates. When the jam oozes, I scoop it with my finger and scrape it off onto the rim of my mug.

There are noises at the front of the house as the first guests arrive and my niece and nephew lope downstairs to greet them. Amidst the shrieking, I hear fake bright voices of fathers coaching their kids to be good, to be polite, to remember their allergies and when they'll be picked up.

Maybe I can't do this yet.

I am staring at Sara's lima-bean project, fetus-shaped, in the bottle by the window, fingering the withered leaves hanging from a spider plant. I need a cigarette a drink a hug a joint a good fuck a man who doesn't—

Okay. Breathe. Forget it. Focus. Clean up the crusts. Wipe off the counter. Just keep doing what you're doing.

Karen takes the sandwich plates and kicks open the swinging door into the dining-room with a flourish and a strained but cheerful, "Okay, kids, come and get it. This is lunch."

A few minutes later I kick open the swinging door myself and take a look. The kids are screaming, lunging across the dining-room table, over each other, grabbing, shouting. My brother-in-law, George, is standing away from the table looking bemused and helpless. Karen darts back and forth shouting into the ears of the kids, asking them to make their requests for sandwiches right into her ear. The noise is deafening.

"Hey kids, can you guess who I am?"

This is my voice, very clear, and around it is silence. They are all looking at me, sizing up my grey-flecked hair, the circles under my eyes, the thickness under my sweatsuit. "Sara, Joey, don't tell. See if they can guess." God, I pray, don't let them say that I am someone's mother.

A boy at the corner of the table—later I learn his name is Benjamin—says, "I know. You're Sara's aunt. She told me."

I cannot believe these kids are quiet. Karen and George are staring at me. My voice continues. "I was wondering. You see I don't know a lot of kids myself. I was wondering if you could tell me some jokes."

Benjamin shouts, "Sheldon knows the best jokes in the class." As I try to find Sheldon among the upturned faces, a girl beside me tugs my arm and looks up at me through red pus-filled eyes smeared with ointment. Her face looks incredibly old and pitiful. "Don't let Sheldon tell jokes. He tells dirty ones about bare naked bums and"—a pause—"you know what."

"Shut up, Penny, you're always telling on me. You like the dirty jokes more than anyone in the class."

For the next fifteen minutes, I make peace, monitor the jokes as the boys try to sneak in their young distorted versions of sex under the guise of something else—"There was this priest, minister and rabbi—" and the girls sit and watch them, titillated and huffy. Penny slouches in her chair, sniffing.

Back in the kitchen, Karen is amazed. "How did you do it? You tamed them. They love you." Suddenly she looks uncomfortable. There is a live wire, it is me, jumping at random around the room. Whatever she says burns us both. I back off.

Sara's birthday cake is a baroque affair made by Karen. When we were children, she was always better with details. Where I would paint in huge strokes, often brooding skies streaked with grey or black, she would border her pictures with hundreds of flowers and remain crying over smudges long after I had abandoned her and gone onto something else. The cake is a lopsided, round, bulbous structure like a messy Orthodox church, stuck around with jelly beans and raisins. Karen asks me to take the cake into the dining-room.

Karen has hired the two girls next door, older by a few years, to conduct some games. She divides the kids into two groups, sends half of them upstairs with the neighbour girls for a treasure hunt and brings the other half into the kitchen for arts and crafts. The boys want no part in either activity. They form their own group and move into the den where they play a boring game called Babar quietly and civilly for the next hour.

"I should have bought finger paint." Karen is trying to

prepare the arts and crafts—little white plaster of paris moulds that are supposed to harden quickly so that the girls can paint them, stick magnets on the back and, Karen tells me, "take them home to put on their mothers' refrigerators."

Each mould is different, and already the girls are clambering up to the counter, picking their own, making deals with me, elbowing each other out. "There's enough for everyone," I say automatically. I am surprised at how automatically my words came out, because there are not enough to go around. The girls realize this a moment after I do, and they push against me, stretching their necks up to my face, each trying to elicit some promise of favouritism from me. Somewhere else I am longing to sit down because inside me everything is aching, but I'm engrossed in their struggle. They have to fight to get what they want. No, not fight. Bribe. Cajole. Extort promises. Their young faces distort like witches. Among them I notice Daniella, a frail, porcelain-doll girl who has circled her arms around my hips and is rocking me back and forth, saying, "Please give me one. Give me one." The instructions read that we should wait for twenty minutes for the plaster to set. The girls nag at me, and after fifteen minutes we begin to release the moulds.

When the girls start to paint, the plaster of paris forms, too soft when I released them, crumble damply. The girls lash out at me, all their sweetness gone, that it was my fault. I fight back, defending myself. "I wanted to wait. Don't blame me. Don't blame me. Don't blame me." The words echo strangely in my head, running together until I force them to stop.

I promise a second batch of moulds, and convince the girls that they'll have to wait until they harden. I hate them now, carelessly promise the same mould to three different girls, run my hand down my arm to free myself from their leeching grasp, repeat over and over, "They were too soft before. They broke. You have to wait till they harden." The pain in my belly is becoming sharper, so that I back down and let them release the fragile moulds themselves. They are blind to the science of it; the moulds are not ready, they will break too.

When the girls realize that this second batch has failed too, they start to wail. Not at me, not at each other, but a strange howling to no particular ear. I turn away and hold onto the counter against the pain. The autumn leaves are swirling over the deck. On a table outside Karen has left some discarded gourds. Breathe. Focus.

Behind me I hear a little voice, chanting as if she's talking to a doll. "Look, I'm taking the broken ones, the ones no-one wants, and I'm painting them. I've got lots. The broken ones are good too." It is Daniella, the tiny porcelain-doll girl.

Tears are shooting into my eyes. The girls are looking at me, and I dry my face with my sleeve and push aside a bunch of hair that got loosened from its elastic at the back of my head. In the silence surrounding us I sniff, "Daniella, that's good. I like what you're doing."

I'm over at the sink again, busying myself with washing up, watering the plant that doesn't need it, staring at the abandoned deck. The tears are flowing freely now, tears for all the broken ones, for earth's soft unripe fetuses that die in wombs, for unfairness and for the small salvation of the broken ones that Daniella has brought to me, unbidden.

Someone is pulling at the elastic of my pants. It's Penny, the one with the sore, runny eyes. Her lips are twisting so that I can barely make out what she is saying. I move my ear close to her lips and I hear her hissing, small voice. "She's lying. Daniella's lying. She's not taking the ones that other people made. She's breaking them herself, and painting over them. She's got more than anyone else. And I didn't get any."

Do I know what I'm doing? Daniella is clutching terrified at my sweatshirt. I am shaking her, pulling her hair, shouting at her. I call her a witch, she broke them herself, they weren't broken before. The boys come in from the den and stand at the doorway, staring silently with their mouths open. Until Karen pushes past them, actually stepping between Daniella and me and shooing the others out of the kitchen.

I wait for Karen to commiserate with me as I tell her, "Don't you see the unfairness everywhere? She broke the other ones. How many did she need? Some of them didn't get any. And they watched her doing it. They watched her stealing them." I am sitting in a kitchen chair with my elbows pressed into my knees. Karen stands quiet and hard and says, as if I am a child, "Clean this up. The parents are coming. Control yourself."

I sniff and ask her what I should do with the broken pieces.

"I don't care," she says. "Throw them out. Do it fast."

I am alone in the kitchen, still crying, but softly this time, like a summer fountain. My breath is easy and rhythmic. I roll the newspapers, folding the debris of the afternoon into them. In their flight from the kitchen, some of the girls have left tiny perfect little painted forms behind. There are flowers, a sheep, some half moons. I roll them into the newspaper too. I sweep the floor and edge the pieces of plaster over the lip of the dustpan as if this is important work. I stand for a while in front of the window and watch the leaves moving over the deck floor. In the distance, I hear adult voices as parents come to pick up their kids. I will stay here in the kitchen until everyone leaves. Then I will go to see Sara's presents.

MARINA ENDICOTT

Mount Misery

When I drank gasoline at the top of Mount Misery, Mr. Anderson ran me down the mountain and saved my life. It was not such a lot of gasoline, but it tasted terrible and they all thought I was poisoned to death. It was not such a big mountain, either, but he ran quickly, holding on to my hand, and leaped sometimes, pulling me with me with him lightly.

Mr. Anderson had been cutting down trees nearby (like the good woodcutter from the story, busy with his work while Apollo watches). His two daughters yelled for him as soon as I started to cough and spit. They were glad to yell and stop the game, which they hadn't been understanding. So instead of becoming a god, which was the point of drinking from the hollow in the sacred stone at the very summit of the mountain, I got run down the stony paths and straight into the Anderson's garage. The others stayed up there, not playing any more, but waiting for me to come back alive.

Mrs. Anderson was not home, she was probably shopping.

"Rinse out your mouth with this," he said. "Spit in here."

"Some of it went down."

"Keep rinsing, I'll be back in a minute."

He disappeared into the house. I didn't know exactly whether to follow him into their kitchen or stay in the garage, so I stayed.

My mother always told me about when she was small and went to stay with a friend, and their bathroom was right at the top of the basement stairs. One morning she was playing hide-and-seek with her friend and she yanked open the basement door to hide there, and there was her friend's father sitting on the toilet with the door open. He just smiled and nodded, but my mother never got over the horror of it, the intrusion she had made. He looked so little, she would say, sitting on the toilet with his pants around his ankles. Mr. Anderson could run me all the way down the mountain without his breath changing, and I didn't want to see him looking little.

Their garage was clean and tidy, nothing out of place and nothing that looked useless. I spat into the sink some more—they had a concrete sink in the garage—and swilled water around my cheeks. I could taste it up in my nose. It had looked so beautiful in the rock: blessed, waiting on purpose for me to come there to drink it and be transformed into God. The gasoline gave the water a purple cast, swirled with green, like on rainy roads. Holy water should be that way.

Mr. Anderson came back with a glass of milk and a piece of bread and honey. He let me drink the milk and didn't talk to me. He sat on the fender of his car with both his feet on the ground and his hands on his knees, and waited patiently until I drank it all. Then he went back into the house.

Our garage was always filled with strange sticks and bits of appliances, old cribs, boxes marked SEWING, GIVE AWAY. But you could get into the rafters in our garage quite easily, and it still smelled of straw from when it had been a stable. I didn't think Wanda and Winona, Mr. Anderson's daughters, would ever climb on the rafters in any garage.

He was not like his daughters or his wife. They were small and dark in that tidy way, their hair always fell in the same direction and looked shiny, and they never talked loudly. Mr. Anderson was big and medium-brown everywhere, like dust. He came back with another glass of milk.

"Feeling better?"

"Yes, thank you."

"Someone must have been trying to set a fire up there."

"On Mount Misery?"

"Is that what you call it?" He didn't laugh, I didn't think he was laughing at us. "There's always some crazy around, someone's been trying to set the mountain on fire for a while. The patch behind the church where the blueberries are, that was a fire, but we caught it before it got too far. Blueberries always grow better where there's been a fire, did you know that?"

"No," I said. I had finished my milk, and I handed him my

glass, but he didn't move right away.

"I guess you better tell your mother you drank gasoline and lived, eh? Did they dare you to do it?"

"No, I did it myself."

"Didn't you smell it?"

"I thought it was rainwater."

"From now on always smell things before you drink them, eh?"

I thought Wanda and Winona were very lucky to have a father like that and I wished my father would say practical things like that instead of the things he did say. But then I thought, he *would* give me advice except he believes I can figure it out for myself. But he wasn't big and dusty like Mr. Anderson.

He took the glass from me and went in again.

"You can come too, you know," he said.

So I followed him up the two steps from the garage and into their house, empty and clean like the garage—Mrs. Anderson not home, the house empty of her. The kitchen was immaculate. He rinsed out the glass and dried it, all easily and quickly, although the kitchen looked much too small for him.

While we were talking in the garage he'd looked right at me, and talked right to me, but inside the house he didn't talk at all, or look in my direction, so I could look around.

Wanda and Winona were the most boring girls we knew, we never played with them on purpose. Once we did, because their house was beside a field, and one winter morning we woke up and there was hoarfrost all over, and I wanted to go over to the field where no-one had walked yet and make mysterious designs in the snow. We thought we should knock on their door first, since it was their field. They were so ordinary, though, they wrecked everything. Because they were there, Cecy and I found ourselves performing for them, talking about a Winter Wonderland and the Snow Fairies. They made everything less than it could be.

Mr. Anderson finished with the glass. It made a still, heavy sound when he put it back in the cupboard. We walked back through to the garage, me still following him, trying to be as quiet as he was. Like robbers in someone's house while the people were there asleep, like servants going through rooms unseen.

Right at the door to the garage, we heard a car pull in. The engine turned off, there was a pause and then the chunk of a door closing. Mr. Anderson had had his hand out to turn the knob. I was surprised to find that it was still out, waiting. Then he opened the door, and there was Mrs. Anderson with two bags and a dress box from Maitlands.

"Oh, hello," he said, taking the bags from her. "Good shopping?"

She didn't even nod, she just walked past us and on into the kitchen. She'd had her hair done, you could smell it strong and sweet on her.

Mr. Anderson went after her with the bags, into the kitchen, and I could hear him talking quietly to her, but not her replying. After a minute he came back.

He said, "I'll walk you back up. Not many people drink gasoline and live. Besides, I left my axe up there."

We walked back up the mountain. Cecy and Sam and Tony Salash were still up there, but Wanda and Winona had gone to Libby's house because they didn't want to be associated with us, even while their own father was saving my life. That was fine with me, I didn't like them at all. Probably there were matching mother-and-daughter outfits for them in the Maitlands bag.

Mr. Anderson left me at the top and said we were supposed to watch out for more gasoline in case the arsonists were still at it. He grinned at me, easy again among the trees, and said, "You're all right now." I was, so I nodded. I didn't have to thank him or anything, I thought it would have been rude by that time to say thank you, as if I didn't know him.

Cecy and I had to tell Tony Salash what arsonists meant: he was trying to tell us that it was something dirty, to do with asses. He was supposed to be smarter than we were, so he wouldn't go back into the game properly for a long time. He sat on a rock and asked too many sarcastic questions and the whole thing was ruined.

It rained for the rest of the week, so hard we couldn't play outside. The hollow in the stone must have filled and overflowed so often that the gasoline would be washed out, but the game had only worked that one day. It was the light on the hill that day that made it.

Cecy and I had a long story going with people we cut out of magazines and moved around in countries we'd made on the floor up in the sewing-room. Sam played until we'd finished making the world—he wanted to go back to his maps in his own room. He was working on an impregnable fort with myriad underground passages and was trying to draw a three-dimensional map of it. The weather was perfect for long drawings.

My mother was having a Ladies' Auxiliary meeting downstairs in the rainy dining-room. They were sitting right under the hot-air vent in the sewing-room floor, near the Lake of Discord, a large swath of blue lining where several of our people were sojourning for the summer. Their talk had been a murmuring underflow to the game, and we'd had to be careful to whisper around the vent, which gave an air of conspiracy to the people on the Lake of Discord and made that part of the game the most interesting.

The meeting was finished, but some ladies were still there, so my mother had gone to make more tea. They were talking and talking, and we were whispering above them, not listening, but then someone said, "Wendy Anderson... "

"Where did you hide the Key to Future Joy," Cecy was whispering, being Cardinal Renaldo.

"Shh, shh," I said.

"Only tell, caro mio, no-one will hear—"

"No, shut up—"

She stopped the Cardinal's snaky voice and looked up at me, lying on the floor with her arm stretched out under her ear.

"What?"

It took a minute for our hearing to slide down to the other conversation.

"...down on Barrington Street, near the hotel," one of the women was saying, Mrs. Ross.

"She saw you see her?"

"Clear as day, she gave a jump! I didn't know him, dark-haired man."

"Such a kind man, too, salt of the earth, Phil, he's—"

Then we could hear my mother come back in with tea. They stopped talking in those sweet shocked voices and started in on the tea.

"What? What?" Cecy kept asking me, and, "Where are you going?" when I went out the door.

She followed after me to our room, where the ladies couldn't hear us.

"Didn't you even hear?"

"Yeah, I heard, Mrs. Anderson's down on Barrington Street. Who's Phil?"

"Mr. Anderson's name is Philip."

"So she was down on Barrington Street with her husband and they're getting all whispery about it?"

"Don't be so dumb. He has brown hair, this other guy on Barrington Street had *dark* hair."

"Brown hair *is* dark hair," she said. She was getting mad at me, because she was so innocent and couldn't understand what they were saying. I didn't want to talk about it any more. Half because that would make her even madder, that was the top, piddling reason. But more because it made me very uncomfortable to know anything at all personal about Mr. Anderson and his wife, it made me feel terrible.

"Come back and play," she said, but I wouldn't. I went and sat in the bathroom with the door locked. I should have been enjoying the one time when it was me who wasn't talking, and

Cecy who wanted me to, but I just sat there remembering her dark smooth hair and her Maitlands bags and how she hadn't even said Yes, hadn't even nodded, when he asked her if she had a good shopping trip. I could taste the gasoline back in my mouth, the way it filled all the creases of mouth-skin that I hadn't even known were there, made my whole mouth go spit! spit!

I went back up Mount Misery when it stopped raining. I used to hang around quite a lot by the rain-pool. When it got into pure hot June no-one else wanted to play up there. All our friends and even Cecy and Sam went down by the martello tower and the sea or back in the lake woods where the caves were, so I was alone. One afternoon I even considered setting fire to the mountain so Mr. Anderson would have to run out from his house and save my life again. I even took a book of matches from the drawer in the dining-room sideboard and had them in my pocket for some time. But I was not very good at lighting matches, I was always startled by them even though I knew what was coming, that sizzle—the matches stayed in my pocket. I didn't see any crazies, or anyone at all. Mr. Anderson must have cut all his wood for the summer, because he never came up the mountain.

I don't know what I thought I was going to say to him anyway. Maybe I would have looked at him with sorrow and pity speaking in my eyes or something dumb. I used to practise in the mirror—it makes you sick when you get like that. Only at the time you're doing it, it seems real. It's later when you're trying to go to sleep that it makes you squirm to think about yourself being such a moron, thinking you're so mature.

Mrs. Anderson left in August. She took Wanda and Winona with her, and went to live with her mother in New Brunswick. The ladies talked about it on the stairs down to the church basement before coffee hour, about her leaving without a word or a note and how he had never known what hit him. My mother heard Mrs. Ross beginning and decided we had to go up to the organ loft for a moment to get some music she'd been looking for, so we didn't know anything else.

We went picking blueberries at the end of August. The best place was out by Ocean Drive, behind the new houses being built. Just their bones were together, you could see the plumbing snaking up for the bathrooms and how many bedrooms. I liked to walk around in them and pretend I lived there. Cecy got too bossy though, and I stepped on her foot, and she went away to pick. So I was by myself when I saw Mr. Anderson coming through the backyard of one new house. He had a bucket full of blueberries already. It looked like he'd eaten some, he had purple on his mouth.

I said hello, and he said hello back. Then I did something so stupid—I gave him my hand, with the outside up, like he should kiss it or something. I think I thought I was the queen doing him a favour by saying hello even though I knew his wife had gone without a word or a note and was down on Barrington Street probably right at this minute going into the Uptown Hotel with the dark man. I was still caught in pretending from walking through the houses.

He smiled at me as if I had done him a big favour, but instead of kissing my hand he took an apple out of his shirt pocket, turned my hand the right way up, and stuck the apple in it. "Nice to see you," he said. The apple was warm from his shirt, from his chest.

He was going to keep on walking. I wanted to say something—I said, with him almost turned away, "Can I help you?" Then I thought how sicky-sweet that sounded, like one of the church ladies, so I said, "Pick?"

"You've got an empty bucket of your own," he said. "How do I know you're a good picker?"

"I just got here," I said. "We just came, I pick fast."

He was laughing again, like when I called the hill Mount Misery. "Could you pick me a bucket in a minute?" He made it sound like a task in a story, spinning straw into gold.

I wanted to say, "I could empty the ocean with a sieve!" to match him, but I wasn't sure he'd get it. I took a bite from the apple in case he thought I didn't want it.

"That's a good apple," he said. "It's from that tree." He pointed to the edge of the unmade garden. "This is my new house," he told me. "Come and see."

We walked through it, over the plain new boards that smelled so raw and good, going through the proper door holes even though the walls weren't there yet. We went up the stairs to where the second floor would be, too, but not over the bare beams. I would have if he hadn't been being careful of me. He told me what colour the rooms were going to be. There were four bedrooms, which made me feel queasy like I might cry because he had no-one to put in them any more. I kept seeing the Uptown Hotel sign, it made it difficult to talk.

I'd finished the apple by the time we came down to the empty back door again. Mr. Anderson held out his hand for the core. I'd sucked it dry, so it wasn't such a horrible thing to put in his hand.

He walked down the board steps and paced along the earth, looking up at the apple tree. "There," he said. He dug the heel of his boot into the dirt, and planted the apple core in the hole. "Now I'll have two trees," he said. He stood still—you could see something running through him like sap. He looked happy alone in his garden.

I picked up my bucket again and went down the stairs, I could see Cecy coming across the open field to find me.

"You're a nice girl," Mr. Anderson said when I said good-bye. "Say hello to your mother for me."

I said I would and I smiled at him properly, without all that sorrow and pity stuff that I was doing when I was only imagining him. I ran across his garden and out into the field to Cecy, thinking of something my father said once, golden apples of the sun, silver apples of the moon.

In the spring Mr. Anderson's wife came back. They said she

couldn't do any better for herself so she'd come home to eat crow pie. When I heard Mrs. Ross talking about it I discovered that I'd been imagining the stupidest things, about me suddenly old enough, living in Mr. Anderson's house with him, sitting under the apple trees in the evening while he gardened. I couldn't stand how much of an idiot I was. Of course she would come back, and of course he would want her back, because she was neat and tidy with smooth brown hair and hardly spoke to him. They were still in the old house. I wouldn't go near it in case I had to talk to Wanda and Winona, the goblin girls.

The Sunday after Easter I got to walk home alone—my father had a finance meeting and everyone else was at home sick. Instead of going along the road, I went behind the church and up the hill into Mount Misery, by the old narrow path we never used. I'd forgotten all about the matches and the old weak yearning I used to feel when I was waiting for Mr. Anderson to come to save me again. I was just walking by myself up the narrow places, up the stairs of the rocks sticking out of the pine needles.

It was early in spring, when the snow was first gone and all the old leaves were drying again with that smell they make. I wasn't even filling up the time with thinking about something, I was thinking about everything.

I stopped by the sister rocks where the water came through into the green pool; I thought I would sit there and look at everything.

The place was heavy and still. In the middle of the big rocks there was a strange flat area filled with moss. The game of becoming a god might have worked better there than at the top of the hill. While I was thinking how we could do it again when the leaves came out, but better, I heard someone coming, so I slid back around the bigger rock and crept up to where I could see.

It was Mrs. Anderson walking by herself up the hill. She

walked slowly, with her arms crossed, and at each step she hit her fist against her chest. Her face was clenched up, she kept opening her mouth as if her jaw hurt. She kept straight on going. I don't think she noticed the rocks, the scenery. I think I could have been standing right there and she wouldn't have seen me.

She looked terrible. Her hair instead of smooth and shining was flying away, thin; her mouth was held quiet partly by her fingers going to the edges, keeping guard on it. Watching her from the top of the rock, I could see very plainly that I didn't know anything about her life, or about Barrington Street, or the Uptown Hotel.

The way she was alone made my aloneness, and Mr. Anderson's aloneness in his garden, seem like company. It made me wonder what her name was.

Wendy, that was her name, the woman in the dining-room said Wendy Anderson. A wrong name, a name that had gotten her the wrong two daughters and the wrong life. I was ashamed of myself for not knowing her underneath her name. I thought it might take you to the Uptown Hotel with a strange dark man if no-one knew you.

After that time when I saw Wendy Anderson on the mountain, I looked at the girls again, at school, at church. How they were delicate now in their paleness, how their eyes looked frightened under their bangs, their dark hair lay close to their skulls. They often looked sideways at each other. They were shy. This wasn't a recent result of a broken home, I think they had always been this way, but I'd never seen it. I'd always been looking at them from how different we were: how tidy they were, how compact, and how messy and extravagant I was. They didn't get messy now either, like she had been, up on the mountain with her hair disarranged, her fist beating just below the collar-bone. They were only little girls.

My last baby tooth started to wiggle. I would push at it and stick the point of my tongue in the sharp space between the

tooth and the gum, but it didn't come out. Finally it got to the
stage where other people could see it moving, and my father
offered to tie a string around it and yank it out, but I wouldn't
let him. He wasn't very good at things like that. Sometimes
he would take four or five pulls because he didn't want to hurt
us. One big pain and no more would have been fine, but not
that kind, tentative tug over and over.

The loose tooth got me crazy. My mother said she was going
to take me to the dentist if it wouldn't come out. Everything
was jerky and wrong. My grandfather came to stay, and
bought me a bicycle, dark green with white rubber guards on
the handle-bars. They took my picture riding it in the hall—
that whole time was like riding your bicycle in the hall, it
drove you crazy. Everything was jiggling inside me, this
unbearable feeling of being stuck but constantly moving, no
relief anywhere. Everything felt like my tooth, hanging by a
thin tough thread inside, any outside thread too frail to break
it.

Our washer broke down. Instead of going to a proper
washer repairman, my father mentioned it at a church meeting, and Mr. Anderson said he would come over and fix it. So
he came, and there he was in the basement. I had a squirming
feeling in my stomach, my insides, the same kind of desperate
jangling wanting. Even after seeing Mrs. Anderson alone, I
still wanted to see him.

I went down the basement stairs slowly as if I didn't know
he was there. He had his head in the washing-machine, but he
heard me anyway and looked up. I went down the rest of the
stairs and stood near the washer, just standing around in my
own laundry-room, that was not pushing yourself forward
unbecomingly.

"Drink any more gasoline?" he asked me seriously.

"No, I always smell it now," I said.

He went on working. He was trying to get something out
of the bottom of the washer with a long pair of pliers. There
must have been something stuck. He was too big to get inside

the washer easily, he had to cram in one shoulder at a time.

At the back of his neck his brownish hair curled into rings from the heat. Even his neck was big. He had on the plaid shirt, pretty old and worn out, and a pair of green pants like they wear at Esso stations. I didn't know you could buy pants like that, I thought he must have worked at an Esso station once. I could feel myself getting all soft and stupid, I really liked him. After his garden, being happy alone, and now his wife was back but walking in the woods hitting herself—it almost made me want to cry, not just for him, for her too, even for me. It was all the jiggling in the world, everything was wrong.

"I have a loose tooth," I said. People often like to hear about loose teeth.

"Let me see," he said, bringing his head back up out of the washer.

I leaned my head back and opened my mouth—he was so tall I leaned my head back quite a lot to give him a good view. He put out his hand and held my chin to get a better look, and then he reached up with the other hand and clicked my tooth out with the pliers.

"That one," I had been going to say.

There was my tooth in the pliers.

"There it is," he said. "Put it under your pillow."

I stared at him. How could he do that to me, put his hand casually on my chin and prink out my little tooth like that without warning me about it? How did he dare to do that? But it hadn't hurt one bit, in fact it felt quite pleasant and a relief, so how could I complain? Only it was my *tooth*, and my *mouth*.

He had probably thought about it, considered it slowly and justly, and realized that it was not going to hurt, and probably even knew that my father took four tries on a string and a door, and he was doing me a kindness, even if I got mad. But did he consider that I might say no? I couldn't decide whether to get mad or not.

"Thank you," I said, and I walked toward the stairs.

"Okay," he said; he stuck his head back in the washer. He was practically a servant. He was big, big, brown as dust, and if I had had a little apple to give him I would have polished it on my chest and put it in his hand.

Being Mary

When I was six my mother grew ill. She and my father sat in the living-room, in the same attitudes that they sat in for telling us about new babies coming. For a moment when we went in to sit down with them to be told something I thought it was a baby, but they were sitting very still and they held our hands, which they wouldn't have bothered doing if it was something good. And the doctor had come to our house in the morning, which he had never done for a baby. My mother said that she had discovered that she was sick, that she had cancer, and that she would have to go away for an operation, just before Christmas. This meant very little, really, except that when people had cancer they died. All my relations who had died (none of whom I had known at all well) had died of cancer, it was like a necessary first step in dying.

My father looked quite frightened. He was moving his lips a little, not the internal-praying way, but the biting way. He was holding my hand, and he kept pressing it a little and letting go a little.

I could not help thinking about other things while they were talking, and I may have missed something. I was thinking about playing orphans-on-a-raft, which was then, and remained for many years, our favourite game. On the raft, one of the poor children was always very ill (usually my sister Cecy), and one was weak with hunger and went mad later, and one was strong and pulled everyone else through, except for the ill one, who sometimes died and was a ghost for the rest of the game, giving advice. There were obviously important things about playing that game that I was going to have to take seriously soon—as I was the oldest, I would in real life have to be the strong one (although in the game I sometimes insisted on being the sick one, because I liked dying and giving advice, and also the sick one was usually the one the others all liked the best, which was why she was dying, of course).

They didn't say anything about dying, or about us being orphans. It was, I suppose, a leap for me to think of us as orphans when only my mother was ill, but my mother and father were one thing to me then and my mother was the stronger element in that one thing. They didn't talk about our guardians as they had when they flew in a plane all the way to Montreal without taking us with them. Our guardians were richer than we were, and had six children already, and ran their house like a boot camp, but the mother was spare and grey and elegant and I admired her, and I liked her children.

The part I almost missed, which I didn't understand for a minute, was that this time we were going with them, to Vancouver, for the operation. They explained that we would stay in different people's houses, because there were too many of us for one family (except for our guardians, I suppose, who had so many that they wouldn't notice four more). This was fine, it was always interesting to stay in strange houses—but we were leaving at the end of the week.

We could not leave at the end of the week, because at school I was in a pageant, and I was Mary.

It would have been inappropriate to say so in the quiet living-room. My mother finished telling us about who we would stay with, and my father prayed for a minute, and then we made supper and ate at the pull-down table in the kitchen, which was a treat.

I had never been Mary before, even though I was the minister's eldest daughter and surely an ideal candidate. When the school photographer took our pictures he called me cupcake, which made me sneer at him, and the picture still sits on my mother's dresser, a girl in a beautiful blue dress, with curled hair, sneering in a very pompous way.

My baby sister had been *Jesus* the year before in the church pageant, while I was only an angel, and my brother was the littlest shepherd who got to give his crutch to the baby, but although I knew that the part of Mary was written for me, no-one would cast me. Then I went to school and began to get an education, and to learn to read, which was my spiritual home, and along came Miss Saddlemeyer and let me be Mary.

I also wanted to be Mary because she was truly beautiful and a lovely person and an angel talked to her, and then her baby was God, and when the angel came and talked to her, which must have been a bit surprising, she said, Behold the hand-maid of the Lord, which I thought was the most beautiful thing anyone had ever said. If I had been a boy, I would perhaps have wanted to be God, but for women, in the Bible, there aren't that many parts. Mary Magdalene I felt I needed more worldly experience for.

Things are very unfair too, and some people have to be Jezebel and Martha and Judas and poor Leah, the unwanted older sister, and I didn't want to fall into that kind of thing in real life, and you can see how easy it would be.

It was still inappropriate to say anything about the pageant at night, and in the morning. It was clear that I would have to tell my teacher myself that I would be unable to be in the pageant. But when I got to school it was very busy, and I had to wait until lunchtime. At lunch, Miss Saddlemeyer rushed off to the staff-room right away instead of staying to talk to people and leaving slowly as she usually did, and I went and ate my lunch with Jamie (whose parents were our guardians) just as usual.

Only before I went, I passed a desk with an eraser sitting on it, just sitting there. It was a beautiful pink eraser, not the ordinary kind, but a new kind that smelled wonderful, like candy. I had always wanted to have one of those erasers, to bite into it to see what it tasted like. I put out my hand as I passed the desk, and picked up the eraser, and put it into my pocket.

While we had lunch, I told Jamie that I was going away soon, but I didn't say how soon. I told him that my mother was sick, and he was very impressed. His mother never got sick. When she had had her last baby she did sit-ups the next day and lost all the weight she had gained in three weeks. My mother had once spent three months in bed, being quite sick, and it gave me an edge over Jamie beyond the ordinary edge of being a girl and being smarter and being the daughter of the minister. And when we had eaten our sandwiches (mine was tomato and lettuce, my father's favourite kind, which always got wet during the wait before lunch), I took a bite of the eraser.

It tasted dreadful. Even when I was much older, whenever I was conscious of having done something that I ought to have left undone I got the taste of that eraser in my mouth. It was a terrible cheat, to smell so good and taste like that. It also crumbled in my mouth, so it was difficult to get all the little pieces out without Jamie seeing me. I had to go to the bathroom on the way to our room and rinse my mouth out with warm water. When I got back, Darlene was sitting at her desk looking for her eraser.

She put up her hand when Miss Saddlemeyer came into the room.

"Miss Saddlemeyer, someone has taken my eraser," she said, very loudly. She was an awful girl, with smooth blond hair that separated into strands, and many different pink sweaters. She was quite pretty, but I didn't like her at all, and I was not sorry that I had bitten her eraser into two halves and spit half out in crumbs. Only it would be very awkward if she discovered I had taken her eraser, because she would make a stink. And underneath that objective thought was the certainty that I would go to prison, and underneath that subjective thought was a devastating knowledge that a person who stole erasers and ate them was unfit to be Mary in the play.

Miss Saddlemeyer told her to look again for her eraser, and began writing on the board. Darlene looked on the top of her desk again, but it was not there, of course, because what remained of it was in my pocket, and weighed a lot. Then she turned around to the desk I shared with Jamie, behind her, and looked straight at me, and said quietly, because she didn't want Miss Saddlemeyer to hear her, "You stole it."

Jamie was appalled, and put his fist in her face, which was not the thing to do at school. But Darlene was too mad to tell on him.

"You stole my eraser," she said again to me, "and I know it."

There was no possibility of a quick retort. Darlene was smarter than I thought, and probably God had told her who took her eraser. I couldn't think of anything to say at all, not even: No I didn't. It was a good thing that Jamie was there, because he said it for me, and he said it again, and louder. I was afraid if he kept saying it Miss Saddlemeyer would hear, and as soon as she looked at me she too would know that I had taken the eraser, and a little movie would run in her head of me putting out my hand and taking the eraser, and then me in the lunch-room taking a bite of the eraser, and she would be miserable, because she really liked me, and it is not possible to like someone who takes people's erasers and eats them.

Darlene was getting pinker, and something had to be done, and done properly, or disaster would be upon me, and I would be known everywhere no longer as the daughter of the minister, but as the thief.

"Thief!" she said, still fairly quietly, but people around us were beginning to look.

I looked up at her and said, "I didn't take your eraser." I said it to shut her up forever, to make it impossible for her ever to speak again, to sew her mouth shut, to rob her of the gift of language, and to make her believe me. It was one of the most important things I had ever said, and it was a lie. I put my hand on the eraser in my pocket, and I thought about God, and about jail, and about Miss Saddlemeyer, and I looked at her as if she was a squashed bug who was a liar and a thief herself. It worked very well.

Then I thought about God some more, and I thought that it would be impossible to believe in God if a person could lie and make people believe so easily when she had her hand on the eraser in her pocket and the taste and smell of it still in her mouth and nose.

Darlene sat down in her seat again and looked for her eraser.

Jamie looked at me and twirled his finger around near his ear and then pointed at her, to say: She's crazy. I looked at him and thought how stupid everyone in the world was, and then I walked up to Miss Saddlemeyer's desk and stood there while she finished writing on the board.

If I hadn't taken a bite out of the eraser I would probably have said something. Or I would at least have slipped it onto the floor so she could find it. But stealing an earaser to eat is difficult to confess to, and you can't give one back casually when it is bitten in half, with teethmarks. I thought about telling Miss Saddlemeyer while I waited for her, but it seemed to me that it would serve no useful purpose, and that I was not going to be Mary in the play anyway because I had to go away, and so I wouldn't have to quit from sin, I could quit from absence. I have been unable to live in one place more than two years ever since. Something always comes up that makes it seem better to quit from absence.

Miss Saddlemeyer finished writing on the board and came to sit down at her desk, and I told her I had to tell her something, and she said, "Can you tell me later? I have something important to tell everyone in the class." I would probably have rushed ahead with it anyway, except for having stolen the eraser. I couldn't really bear to be in Miss Saddlemeyer's presence, having done such a thing, because she was the queen of the world to me, so I went back to my desk and sat down beside Jamie again. Darlene was still poking through her desk for her eraser.

Miss Saddlemeyer stood in front of her desk and looked at everyone, and she said. "Would some of you please come out into the hall with me? Put your heads down on your desks. It's a secret."

Then she walked down the aisles and patted people on the head to tell them to come with her. She patted about ten people, I guess, and they went out into the hall, and they were gone for a few minutes, and then they came back and sat down again, and she patted other heads, and went out into the hall again, and she did that several times, but she never patted me on the head. Jamie was one of the first people who went out into the hall. When he came back he looked at me before he put his head back on his desk. I knew he looked at me, but I didn't look up quickly enough to see how he was looking. Darlene went in the third or fourth batch.

Finally Miss Saddlemeyer brought the last batch into the room, and said, "Is there anyone I haven't picked?"

I was about to cry, even though I hadn't cried about my mother being very ill, or about being so bad that I could steal an eraser and then lie so well that everyone believed me. I put my hand up.

"Oh!" said Miss Saddlemeyer. "Of course! Come with me, and I will tell you."

She took me into the hallway, all by myself, and she put her arms around me, and she said, "We heard that you were going away."

Then I did cry, and I said, "I can't be Mary in the play."

She sat down on the floor and pulled me down beside her, and told me that there was going to be a party for me going away, at school, on Thursday. She said we would play games and sing, and she would bring her guitar, and that there would be things to eat, and that we would do the pageant for the class then, which would be a good practice for the other people, and a chance for me to do it once before somebody else was Mary.

I knew what she was going to say just before she said it, which I often did. She said, "Maybe you could help me think of who could be Mary instead?"

I also knew what she thought I would say. There was a girl in our class who was too big for her age, called Karen, who nobody liked very much, not for any reason. Miss Saddlemeyer had made it clear that *she* liked Karen, and that anyone who was mean to her was going to have to explain themselves well.

I understood this, and also that Karen was actually quite nice. Miss Saddlemeyer wanted me to say Karen, who was not in the play at all because she had a broken ankle and couldn't walk much when it was cast, but now she was a bit better, and she would be able to do it.

However, if you are going to steal erasers and not give them back because they are bitten, and then not say anything about having done it and not explain that you should not be Mary because you are not up to it morally, then you have to have your own set of morals. And although I hated Darlene like poison just at that moment, Darlene was not in the play either, because Miss Saddlemeyer did not like her very much, although she didn't show that except by being a little bit nicer and slower with her. Darlene's eraser had been taken and eaten by me, and she would have to be Mary. It was not entirely Darlene's fault that she was so awful. She had an awful mother. Maybe being Mary would be better for her than for Karen, who Miss Saddlemeyer already liked. And if Miss Saddlemeyer knew as soon as I said her name that I had stolen Darlene's eraser, then she would have to know.

"Darlene," I said to her, still sitting on the floor with her arm around me. "I think Darlene should be Mary now."

She was quite surprised, I think. She just sat there for a minute, and then she tightened her arm around me and looked at me, and then she said. "Okay. Darlene it is. You don't have to worry, you know."

She was talking about the eraser.

After school I walked home with Jamie until we went different ways, and then I carried on by myself. I didn't want to walk the usual way, I thought I would have an adventure and walk through other streets.

Darlene had been very surprised too when Miss Saddlemeyer asked her if she would be Mary when I was away—Miss Saddlemeyer was a very good woman, and did not say, "Laura thinks you should be Mary." She must also, I think, have been quite a moral woman, if she could understand what I was doing, and a generous and intelligent one, to say to me only that I didn't have to worry.

There was a lot of snow. It was dark, too, at four o'clock. Not deep night dark, but evening. I walked along the sidewalk of a street one over from where I usually walked. The sidewalks are little valleys when the snow is that high, and it piles on the road side and the house side, and you can't see much but snow, with little yellow pee patches on it from dogs, and holes punched in the banks sometimes from someone trying to climb over to get to the street.

At one corner, though, the snow was cleared away well, and across the street you could see the houses right down to the foundations. One of the houses was burning.

There must have been noise of firetrucks before I saw the house, but I don't remember it. Only coming out of the snow valley into the black street, with a house on fire. People were standing around it, back a little from the flames, watching the house gradually blacken and smoke pour up into the sky.

When you are quite young, six, I was, you know things are important before you learn about symbols. It was a terrifying thing, this fire gulping up the house, waving its arms around and flailing at the beams, but also clean and wintry and beautiful.

I stood and watched it; nobody saw me standing there to tell me to go away.

I was ashamed of taking Darlene's eraser, but it was not after all the crime of the world. I threw the eraser into the fire; it was a good throw and went right into the heart of a window burst open.

I was not going to be Mary, but I would be careful not to be Leah or Martha either. Perhaps I would wait a while and be Mary Magdalene.

My mother was not going to die. Not with a fire like this going on, not when she was so busy, not when her oldest daughter still didn't know everything she needed to know.

I thought with a small regret of the orphans on the raft being self-sufficient and strong and making their own way in the world. Then I turned around and ran home through the snow, in the wind, with the fire behind me.

The Orphan Boy

When people were unhappy, they often came to our house with food. Sometimes they came secretly and left something on the back porch, a pie, a lemon loaf or (one wonderful time) a bucket of fried chicken. At Christmas, big laundry hampers full of cans and bottles of exotic food and drink. But Ariadne Keller came in the middle of the night and pounded on the door and they let her in—how could they help it? She was a tornado standing on the front porch, laughing through the little pane of glass, snapping the knocker back and forth and beating time with her heels, too.

My room, the room the Cecy and I shared then, was right over the front porch. But we had not been asleep, of course, we had been lying in bed arranging our hair on our pillows for the delectation of the Arabian Knight who was going to leap through the window on his charger and carry us off—one knight each: we had got into an argument that evening over whose knight would arrive first, and I was feeling dreadfully certain that mine would be late, and I would have to watch Cecy lifted up into arms of steel and plumped delicately down, sidesaddle. Then there would be that spring, the hind legs of the horse swelling downwards to rebound upwards into the air forever, no need of a magic carpet, and me left alone in our maiden bedroom waiting for who knows how long, covered in humiliation. So when the noise began, the pounding and the rapping and the heels on the wooden porch floor, I was glad enough to disarrange myself and beat Cecy to the window.

"It's Ariadne Keller," I whispered back to her. We always called her by her full name when we talked about her, because my mother did, as if her name was a spell and couldn't be left unfinished. It does sound melodramatic, but so was she melodramatic. Cecy shivered in bed and pulled the blankets back up; they had lain in romantic dishevelment awaiting the shining one.

88

"What's she doing?"

"I don't know yet, she's dancing, I think."

Cecy scrambled up, stamping on the giveaway board, but that wouldn't matter with all the noise.

"Let me see a little."

Ariadne Keller was calling through the door, "Little pigs, little pigs, let me come in!"

That was a little scary and I began to hope that she would go away, but my father was switching on the lights and letting her in. It was his job, of course, to give succour and sanctuary.

My mother stood at the top of the stairs fully dressed by the time Cecy and I worked up the courage to edge our door open a crack. Without turning around to look at us she said, "Back to bed, girls, I mean it."

But Ariadne, coming into the bright hallway with parcels and packages in her arms, looked up the long angle of the stairs and lit up her brilliant eyes at us, and cried, "Oh, no, let them come down too—look at all this I've brought! You can't be so cruel..."

What was my mother to do? My father standing behind Ariadne with his arms out for her things, us waiting for the word, the baby beginning to make little cranky noises, even my brother, who slept a frozen man waiting for medical developments, had come sliding out of his door.

"Robert, it's nearly midnight..."

Cecy and I looked at each other with wild surmise—that was practically a capitulation.

"I should be taken out and beaten, I know," said Ariadne Keller, bowing her long body in shame. "But look what I've brought you! Spaghetti!"

She dropped a bag on the carpet in the hall and began pulling things out of it: long, long spaghetti, longer than we ever got, in a blue and white paper bag; jars and tins, and bunches of garlic, a beautiful string bag full of onions and peppers, a long stick of white bread and a pound of butter, cheese in wrapping, a bottle of wine.

My mother turned around and looked at us. She looked a little pinched and tired, but she smiled. "Are you hungry still?" she asked us. She put out an arm to my brother Sam, and he walked into her. "Hungry, Sam? Spaghetti?"

"They'll be sick for the rest of the night, Ariadne," she said as she started down the stairs.

Real spaghetti, not just out of a can, was still almost an ethnic food. We were thrilled.

My father shut the door and helped gather up the parcels again and we skipped down behind my mother to help. Ariadne was holding on to my mother's arm, coaxing her into the kitchen, thanking her, waltzing her a little, her hand smoothing up and down on my mother's sleeve or clasping her to her for a minute and then pushing her away again. She's hectic, I thought, like Ruby dying of consumption in that Anne book.

"A party, a party!" she sang as she flung cupboard doors open and shut, hauled out big pots and little pots, snapped the stove on, found the corkscrew. My parents looked at each other, calculating how long she would stay, glad that the dishes had been done that evening, apologizing to each other. Cecy and Sam sat on the bench behind the table, very subdued, but I sat on the stool by the fridge, practically in the middle of all of it.

She stayed until dawn, telling stories and making us all laugh. She taught Sam how to do a time-step, she sucked her spaghetti in through the space in her front teeth, she dazzled my father and hocused my mother, and she gave me secret smiles as if we were the only ones in the world who really understood sophistication. Even Cecy sat on her lap for a while—she hadn't sat on anyone for years. I despised her for doing it, but knew exactly why she let her standards slip. Ariadne carried her upstairs when she fell asleep, her little legs drooping to one side and her head drooping to the other like a broken lily—exactly the effect I worked for when arranging myself for the Arabian to come and take me away.

I followed after them and contented myself with the swing of Ariadne Keller's skirt and the beautiful tendon in her heel that stretched sharply away from the bone at every step. The backs of her legs were beautifully brown and smooth and strong, from dancing, I thought. Her arms, too, were strong and thin and fell into exquisite shapes carrying Cecy, easing her gently around the newel post at the bottom of the stairs, pulling her in closer during the climb, lightly raising her over the end of the bed.

"I long for someone to carry me," Ariadne Keller said to me, pulling the sheet up over Cecy. "Not since I was nine like Cecy. Or someone to swirl me around in the air, you know, like an airplane?"

I nodded, shy to be in the room alone with her except for Cecy sleeping.

"If only someone really big would come along and carry me away I could stand it. As long as there's someone who can pick you up you're still okay, I think.... It's only when you get too tall that you're in trouble. On your own."

"I'm eleven," I said. I could have killed myself for saying that. What a dumb thing to say, it didn't even go with that she had said. Now she would leave.

"It's a strange year," she said, looking at me with her side-long eyes. "Magic. I remember being eleven."

She said nothing for a minute. I tried to think of something to say to keep her there, but nothing came.

"Did you know I have a twin?" she finally said, looking in the little mirror.

"No."

"Well, I do. My dear twin, my second soul, my spirit-mate, Ardith the Beautiful..."

My father looked in the door, carrying Sam. "Sleep now, Laura."

Ariadne Keller leaped off my bed where she had settled for an instant and bowed me into it. Then she stretched her fingers up, up, and grazed her fingers on the ceiling. "Too big to be carried, no-one will come and take me away, my own sister deserts me—how will I live?"

She had forgotten me already, but that was part of her glamour—to be forgotten by her was a privilege.

She went downstairs with my father and they both walked straight into his study without even talking about it. She stayed in there with him for a long time. My mother came upstairs slowly after she cleaned up, and she stood in my doorway for a minute to listen to our breathing. My rhythm didn't change, but she came over anyway and kissed me. Her hand stuck clumsily as she smoothed down my hair and it made me feel desperate, too big for the room. Downstairs we could hear Ariadne Keller crying in the study.

After a little while my mother went to her own room, but the crying noise continued into my sleep.

Sam told me she wanted to adopt a boy, that's why she came over in the middle of the night.

"That's silly, why would she want another boy? She's got six children already." It was hard to believe that she was really their mother, but there were six children at her house and they did look a bit like her. More like her husband, the Commander, who was never there. She didn't act like a mother either—what mother would come to our house and make spaghetti in the middle of the night? What were her children doing then?

Sam said solidly, "I know, but that's why she came. His name is Michael Rowe, and he is three."

"That's not a real name. How do you know all this stuff?"

"Daddy told me."

We were sitting on the bank at the side of the house, the side with no windows, eating cookies that I had said we were allowed to have.

Cecy said, "Why did he tell you without you asking?"

"Because he's the only boy, that's why," I told her.

Sam just laughed and looked ordinary, which was annoying. He was aware of things like that, but not much affected by them.

"Well, why don't *we* get the little boy?" said Cecy. Our parents had tried to adopt a boy to have a brother for Sam, but they didn't have enough money, apparently. But my father was still a good reference for someone who wanted to adopt; being the minister, he looked good on the forms.

I didn't understand yet. "Why does she want one particular boy? I thought you just got what come out of the bin."

"I don't *know*, I said, I wasn't even listening," Sam said, getting up to leave. "Maybe she knew his parents. I'm going to ride the scooter." He left.

"So why would she cry?" I asked Cecy.

"When did she cry?"

"For ages after you were asleep. I was awake."

"Liar."

"It's true."

Even later, Sam wouldn't pump Daddy any more, and although Cecy and I talked about it for a while, we didn't really like talking about Ariadne Keller. She was out of bounds, maybe because she was too powerful. She lived on a street called Whitlock Edge, and my mother called her the Witch of Whitlock Edge when she was being unguarded. My father used to change the poem: "On Whitlock Edge the wood's in trouble," he would say solemnly, and you could tell he was feeling a bit of a devil for laughing at one of his parishioners.

About three months after the spaghetti night, we had our portraits taken. A very good photographer came out from Halifax and set up in our living-room. The dining-room was turned into a dressing-room, and we had to wear curlers all morning. It had been arranged through friends of friends, but we had a songbook filled with the photographer's photographs, and she was obviously the real thing. Cecy and I were very impressed. We watched her from the corner where we were sitting quietly while my mother got the baby ready. Miss Howard strutted around fixing up white umbrellas and reflecting sheets and fancy lamps on tripods, and finally got out her cameras. She paid no never mind to us at all, just got on with her work. When we were ready to sit, she sat us, took some pictures, re-sat us and took more. We changed our clothes and did it again. She took individual pictures and pictures of pairs of us. She had just settled on me and Cecy as the last set of all when the doorbell rang, and my father sent Sam to open it.

The woman photographer was fiddling with the film. She had posed Cecy sitting on a chair and me sitting on the arm of the chair with my arm round Cecy's shoulder and my head over her head.

Cecy didn't even have to move her lips to talk to me. "Maybe I'll be a photographer. I bet she makes lots of money."

"How much is she getting for this?"

"A whole bundle, Daddy's mad about it, but Mommy said it had to be done anyway for the Christmas letters."

There was quite a noise out in the hall.

"It's the witch," Cecy said, squirming suddenly. The photographer's working eye caught her moving.

"Just sit still for six more shots," she said reasonably. "Then you can run off."

She must have decided to make the last ones good pictures by talking to us. Maybe she thought she would put them in a book.

"What's it like, you two, being sisters?" she said, just as Ariadne Keller put her head around the archway from the hall. "You must have special secrets, you two. Do you share a room? I always wanted to have a sister, to have a special friend."

While Miss Howard was talking, Ariadne Keller left her body in place, but bent her head away behind the arch and then bent it back, only when she bent it back she had two heads, both nodding and smiling.

Cecy shrieked and jumped up. Her head banged me in the

jaw and made me bite my tongue so I smacked her and she howled.

My eyes were watering from the pain, but there were certainly two Ariadnes standing in the archway, both laughing. The photographer didn't know what to do—we were older than her normal range of children, I guess, and wouldn't have paid much attention to a sucker or the birdie. My mother arrived and told us both to be quiet.

"I am ashamed of you," she whispered fiercely, pulling the cushion of the chair back into place where Cecy had kicked it out in our fight. "Not only is Miss Howard here, we also have guests. I don't want to hear another word until she has finished and you have changed out of those dresses, is that clear?"

We nodded, keeping our eyes on her to assure her of our goodness—also to avoid looking at the door where Ariadne Keller stood with her twin sister like those photography studios where for an extra dollar you get two prints of each photo.

It was soon over—the photographer didn't ask any more questions about being a sister and was probably glad not to be one herself. She packed up her gear while we put on our normal clothes, and my mother and Sam and my father, who had all changed while Cecy and I were getting done, put out tea in the garden.

When Cecy and I got downstairs again, the living-room was empty of equipment and the house of people. We looked out the balcony window by the boxy fireplace and there they all were, having tea down below on the small lawn. Behind our house was a tiny garden and then a row of big rocks, and past the rocks the swamp began—several acres of marsh and bog, rocks and reeds and muck. It was quite pretty, but the mosquitoes were very bad at certain times of the year, and of course there was a smell. But if the wind was the right way, people could sit in wicker chairs in the little garden not even knowing there was a swamp out there.

Ariadne Keller had brought her sister and also the new

little boy whom we (Cecy and I, and Sam) hadn't seen yet. My parents had been to dinner at her house and he had been "on display" my mother said; she also said he was a very ordinary little boy.

The first thing he did was walk around the rocks and straight into the swamp. Cecy and I, looking over the tops of them all from the balcony, saw him heading for the middle along the tussocks of grass and scrub. He was wearing white knee-socks, and they were streaked and soaked already. We should have raced down and caught him, but in fact we knew he would be all right; it was not a dangerous marsh. Instead we stayed leaning on the rail and watched him.

"How old?" Cecy asked me.

"Three, I think."

"He looks older than that, don't you think?"

I was leaning too hard on my chest, I had to get up, so I swung my leg over the rail and sat balanced on the top. "I think he looks like a changeling, a goblin child."

"And Michael Rowe, that can't really be his name."

"Not possibly—where is his boat ashore?"

That made Cecy laugh, and the adults looked up at us, and my mother gestured for us to come down. Sam held up a plate of goodies. Ariadne Keller and her sister stared up at us from their doubled faces, somehow reproducing even the angle of the glance. And a third of the way into the swamp, the child Michael turned around and looked at us too.

It all made me want to show off, but I couldn't think of anything really good to do, so I just stood up on the railing. Cecy made that little squeak noise she makes when she's scared that always pushes me further, so I did a little soft shoe, prancing along the narrow board. Normally I know this would have been no big deal, but the balcony itself wasn't very safe and the railing was particularly rickety, and we had been expressly told never to sit on it, even. Having stood up, walked, done the little dance, there wasn't much available for a finale—but then the little flash caught my eye out in the swamp. It was the Michael boy's white socks flicking through the air as he fell off a rock into one of the water spaces.

I turned to Cecy to say, "Don't be worried, I've done this before," and then I launched out. It seemed to take a long time to get to the ground, as it always does. I hadn't actually jumped from standing up on the railing before, only from standing outside the railing hanging on with my toes to the little bit of extra platform. The four-foot difference nearly ruined me.

But I landed (on all fours instead of gracefully like the goddess from the machine), without breaking either my bones or the tea set, and set off for the swamp.

I had certainly made an impression. My parents leaped out of their chairs, and my father nearly brained Miss Howard with the camera he was examining. Only Sam caught up with me, though, as I was delicately, quickly bunnyhopping from hillock to hillock, mound to root to stump to rock, to where the orphan boy had gone in.

We stopped short about five feet from him, as if he was an animal and might bolt at a sudden movement. In boring truth he was in no danger of drowning. There was only a foot or so of water. But he was only little, and didn't know how to get himself out of the mire. His pretty suit of shorts and shirt was ruined.

"What's that secret word you use for horses and fairies," I said over my shoulder to Sam. He snorted, because really the little boy did look like a brownie, all filthy and pointed. His nose had stayed clean somehow, and it stuck straight out, and his dark hair drew in swoops all over his scalp. You could see the patterns of its growth, unlike most people's thatches. His skin stretched over his face bones more tightly than usual in little kids, and it gave him a knowing, old look. That look dissolved suddenly as we watched him, though, because he started to cry, and he held out his arms to be picked up. I didn't have much patience with babies and never ever played with dolls or anything sentimental, but he made me feel very sad

97

for him, so I did go over and pick him up. I was big enough to hold him almost comfortably. He got muck all over my t-shirt and pants, but he tucked his head into my neck and wrapped his legs around me, and it made me feel strange—huge, like a terrible, kind giant. Cecy had leaped across the swamp from the other direction, and came up to us just before my father reached us.

"That was just stupid," she hissed at me. "You did that just to show off. Let me hold him."

"Don't be crazy, I've got him!"

She started yanking on his legs and made him stir and murmur, and that made me furious, so I whacked her with my free hand and she fell into the swamp herself. Before she could grab my ankle to pull me in, which she was trying to do, my father got there, and he took the boy from me and told Sam to help Cecy up.

While he was lifting the little boy off me, he looked at me seriously and said, "Really well done, Laura, you could have saved his life. I'm proud of you, sweetheart." He smiled and rumpled my hair up and walked back along the safe path.

Cecy was left wallowing in the mud and scratchy branches. She really hated the swamp, too—for her to come flying over a new path as she had done was a desperate feat. Sam gave her his hand half-heartedly; she ignored him and pulled herself out of the sucking slime by roots and rocks. I don't know why I stuck around—I wanted to follow after the boy and be petted and paraded.

She looked at me as she was clawing out. "You want to watch out, Laura," she said. "You could become a horrible person if you don't be careful. Then you'll be old and no-one will like you and Sam and I won't live with you." By that time she was standing up, dripping, looking even more like a swamp-thing than Michael Rowe had. Her pale hair was slapped to her face with dingy water, and her eyes were frog-jewels.

"What did I do?" I asked Sam. I knew that would annoy her

more.

"I'm going to the barn, do you want to come?" she asked him. He looked back and forth between us for a second, but he would have been a fool to refuse her. She was really mad, and if he sided with me she would be mad for days longer. So he went off with her through the swamp over the path she had cut coming in.

They were both pigs, anyway.

I went back by the safe path. My feet hurt from jumping all that height. It must have been twelve feet with the railing added in. At the head of the path between the two guard stones, my mother was waiting for me.

"We're going to have to have a talk, Laura," she said in her quiet, dangerous voice. Nothing got by her. She put her arm around me, leading me into the garden as if we were the best of friends, and smiled for the guests.

It had only been a second, I guess, since my father arrived back with the kid. He was holding him under the garden hose, rinsing the worst of the black muck off him, and Ariadne and her sister were standing anxiously by, not looking at each other, only at the child. Ariadne rushed forward, dragging her sister, when my mother sashayed me into the garden.

They were both wearing flowered things, long and full in the skirt, made of vague, ghostly cloth that sharpened their own vividness. Some of the colour was paled, though, in both of them. I was surprised to see that they'd gotten so fond of a little orphan boy in just a few weeks—or maybe they just felt guilty about him, like I did about the baby if I dropped her when I was supposed to be babysitting.

"Laura, thank you a million times," she said, but she wasn't really talking to me at all, she kept looking back at the boy. "This is my sister, Ardith. I want her to meet you, she's staying with me for a little while. Ardith, I think you'll love Laura..."

Ardith put out her hand for me to shake, and as soon as our hands touched, Ariadne leaped back to the little boy—it was like the fizzy light leaping between two metal sticks in an electricity experiment. Ardith snapped her head around to watch her sister, but she turned back to me soon enough for politeness—well, more than politeness, because I was only a child anyway, she didn't have to talk to me.

Seeing her out in the garden made it clearer why Ariadne had talked about her so strangely. They were the same, only Ardith was more of it. She turned her eyes on me, and they were so beautiful—slanted and deeply set, with shadows around them. Her hand, still holding mine, was long and veined and well kept, and she had a ring on that glinted. Just one ring, no wedding band.

"I expected to see wings on your shoulders," she said to me. "Wings for an angel, wings for a bird! You must have been practising flying."

"No, but I dream I'm flying," I answered her, and that was a lie—only Cecy ever dreamed she was flying, I never got into the air no matter how hard I tried.

"Oh! So do I, always!" she crowed, and her eyes glinted at me like her ring. For a minute I was glad I had lied about flying in dreams, but then I suddenly thought that she was lying too, that she didn't dream she flew either. "Over cities and towns, like the dark man in Chagall, or like the Queen of the Night." She went on about flying, talking in poetry almost, but she wasn't talking to me at all any more, although her eyes were still on me, keeping me in place. All her concentration was going behind her to Ariadne and the boy.

My mother touched me lightly as she went by, and said quietly, "Change your clothes again, please, and find Cecy." She helped Ariadne clean the last bits of mud from Michael's face.

Ardith said, to call me back, "Before I leave we'll have to take her out for a treat, won't we? Something really wonderful."

I couldn't understand what she meant until I realized she was talking to Ariadne, about me. I only got that because

Ariadne came close, still holding the little boy, with her arms wrapped right around him. She looked at me over Ardith's shoulder, and smiled, and I thought for a minute that she was much more beautiful than Ardith. "Yes," she said, "Oh, yes, we will! What a good idea!"

I took a gulp of whisky once, when I thought it was apple juice. Those women made me feel like that most of the time.

Sitting on the roof of the garage one evening later on, when Cecy wasn't mad at me anymore, we were trying to decide how high the balcony railing was exactly without getting out the measuring tape. Sam was talking about a theory of his to do with shadows and string, and Cecy thought if we got Daddy to walk underneath it by some ruse and then estimated it— her formula wasn't quite worked out. I campaigned fairly hard for the sixteen-foot theory because it was after all me who had jumped off it without breaking anything.

"I bet that Michael kid is her sister's baby, and she's pretending to adopt him," I said.

"No, because Daddy signed the papers."

Sam said, "He did, I was a witness."

H needed to be squashed, he was getting out of hand. "You are only a child," Cecy told him.

"You couldn't be a witness, you silly baby, you're only eight."

"And he's not her sister's baby," he said, getting a little mad. "He's her own, that's whose baby he is, and she got him back, and Daddy thinks it's best that she have him back, and me too."

"What?"

"Really?"

"I just *told* you, do you think I lie or something?" Sam was stalking down the roof to the branch to get off. "You guys are so *old*, well, you don't even remember when she went away to Montreal for a long time and they thought she wasn't coming back but then she did, and I remember that."

"Be careful on the branch," Cecy told him. "Don't jump from too high."

"I know how to do it," he said, but he wasn't really mad any more. "I'll get some graham crackers."

"Bring oranges too if you can," I said, but Daddy caught him going in the kitchen door; we could see them both outlined in light, Daddy bending down and Sam bending up—then Daddy picked him up and tossed him in the air and came out to the porch to call us.

"When they take me for a treat, you can come too," I told Cecy while we climbed down through the dusky air inside the shell of leaves.

They came to pick me up on the second Sunday after Trinity, in June, after lunch. I didn't know they were coming. We were all sitting at the table still. Sam was making us laugh, with his eyes two circumflexes but his mouth straight, not laughing with us. We had our arms on the table to lie on while we laughed, and my mother was gasping with laughter, helpless with it, cutting loose—my father having to wait for a breath before he could add to the joke. The baby was banging with a spoon on her tray and singing—no wonder we didn't hear the car grating on the gravel, we were in our house, laughing.

The first we heard was heels on the step outside the kitchen door and rapping, rattling on the pane, and different laughter coming from outside. Two faces, the same face, and two panes of glass. My mother hiccoughed and nearly laughed again, but she pulled herself up out of what she liked best and whipped the cloth off the table before she opened the door. My father stood up too and put his glasses on. Cecy and I untangled our legs from each other and left the table—she going toward the hall door, me into the middle of the kitchen. Sam stayed at the table; he still had his pudding bowl in his lap to finish.

They came in laughing, but we had all stopped for guests, so they were laughing alone now, and Ardith was singing something.

"We've come to take Laura for her treat," Ariadne said, "If you'll let her come? Ardith wants to see the sea, we're going to drive down the south shore, maybe as far as Chester. But I promise you we'll have her back in time for dinner—let her come with us, please...."

She sounded more like the spaghetti night again, all urgent and flattering, humming like a telephone wire. I think there were sparks of light coming off her, but I may just remember it that way. Ardith, too, still singing, "I want to be, beside the sea..." and both their skirts dancing around their legs, high staccato shoes dancing on our tiles. I wanted to go so badly, I couldn't see anything but the two beautiful women, and my mother standing like a tree in the kitchen, not laughing, but smiling for company. I was afraid to look at her face in case she wouldn't let me go, but she just said, "Run up and put on your warm sweater, Laura, and brush your hair, darling."

I ran before she changed her mind—why should she have changed her mind? To get to the stairs I had to pass Cecy standing in the archway to the hall, and she didn't move when I went by, not even to look at me, but it was worth it. I was the oldest, it was fair, I could get her back later.

When I came down again Cecy was gone and so was Sam, and my mother was in the kitchen with the baby, but no-one else.

She called me back before I was out the door. "I love you," she said. "Be home on time." She held the baby lightly on her lap.

Back into the dark hallway, past the study door (no sound at all, that I could hear). I pushed at my hair in the hall mirror for a minute, but I still couldn't hear anything. No sign of Cecy, they must be in the barn already, but then through the balcony windows I saw her and Sam sitting on the head rock in the middle of the swamp. He was staring toward the house and she was talking to him with her chin stuck out forward, kneeling on the bumpy rock in her bare knees. Too many windows in this house, I thought.

Ardith was sitting in the driver's seat, playing the radio softly and smoking a cigarette with her arm out of the open window. I was a little shy to come up to the car, but she saw me and made me get in the front seat with her.

"Never wear stockings in June, Laura," she said. "Just too hot. Did you know that nylon is an excellent insulation? That's why I always wear stockings in the winter. Your legs stay warm! But as soon as it's summer, I just put them away."

I looked down at my own legs, pale brown and scratched, and I thought of my mother, wearing a girdle and nylons every day of her life, squirming into the tube of gripping in the morning, laughing with us at how silly she looked, folding the edge up to attach her stockings.

Ardith's shins were brown and as smooth as Ariadne's, maybe a little thinner. She stretched them toward me and twisted the ankle to examine it, in her stiletto heel. No-one else would have worn those shoes to go and be beside the sea. "New York, Paris, London—walking through great cities has lathed my legs, Laura," she said (and she said it for poetry). "What am I doing here, is the question I ask myself. She had a brilliant future, you know, she could have done anything—and instead, she lives in a back-water with all those children.... It is sordid, isn't it. Have you read *Brave New World*? You'd love it. Luckily Lisle is old enough now to take care of them sometimes. Thank God I didn't do the same—I look at her life sometimes and just sigh, I just have to sigh—you know what I mean, don't you Laura?"

I nodded. "And now another child," I said, trying to continue the conversation.

"Yes, well, you know all about that, of course, being your Daddy's daughter..." She looked at me as if I was a woman, so I nodded again. "It's an awkward situation, I feel terrible about the whole thing. It doesn't seem to be working out too well, if you want my untutored opinion...so much to feel guilty about! Sometimes I think I will have to take him back. He's a difficult child, I see that, and the Commander doesn't make things any easier." She laughed—I would have to say ruefully, shaking her head slightly.

By this time I was completely lost. It seemed best to just let her think I knew everything, so I rolled down the window on my side and stuck my arm out too. No cigarette, unfortunately. She flipped her envelope bag open beside her on the seat and went through it like a filing-cabinet, looking for something. Her bag matched her shoes, and they were green, the same green as her dress. Her nails were polished coral and flicked over the things in her bag: leather covered books with a purpose, compacts covered in other leather, a bottle of perfume, a gold lipstick. She looked up and smiled at me watching her and a dimple came in her cheek, a tight, perfect dent.

The front door banged, and Ariadne came headlong down the steps. My father was still standing in the door, watching her run. And then she was at the car, opening the front door beside me, and I made to get out and get in the back, but she stopped me.

"No, no, this is a sight-seeing tour! We can all sit in the front. Let's go, Ardith."

Ardith held my knees over toward her to make room. "We'll go and get Michael first," Ariadne said as she slammed the door.

My stomach did a snake thing. I looked at the dashboard. If she was going to bring Michael on this treat I should stop the car and ask to bring Cecy. My legs pinched because I'd pulled my knees together when Ariadne got in, but the underskin had stuck in its old place. Ardith had already backed out of the driveway, and the yellow forsythia bush by the door blocked out my father. Then around the corner of the house I could see Cecy on the rock, by herself now. Sam was probably on the scooter.

"But what about Laura's treat?" Ardith asked the air outside her window. She flicked her fingers on the steering-wheel. I sat still.

Ariadne leaned forward and banged the glove compartment open. "I don't want to leave him with Lisle."

"She's fourteen—she's all right with him."

"Where are the maps?"

"We don't need a map."

They looked at each other for a minute. We had come to the turn-off to St. Margaret's Bay Road, and I sat very still. Then Ardith turned the car to the right instead of the left, and we went to get Michael. If I'd known how, I would have gotten out of the car and walked back to our house.

At Ariadne Keller's house the road curved into the trees, and the land sloped down from the road to a small lake behind the house. They had a dock. Ardith stayed in the car while we walked down the path to the lake. Ariadne Keller ran ahead to where Lisle and Michael Rowe were sitting on a blanket. Lisle stood up when she saw us, holding Michael—they both stared at us with the same expression, something closed and serious.

Ariadne lifted Michael high in the air so his legs spun out and said to Lisle, "I'm taking him with us after all—Laura doesn't mind, do you Laura?" She was all sparkling again, and she smiled, but she looked so unhappy underneath it that I didn't really mind. "Just wait while I get his runners..." she flew up the path to the house.

Lisle folded up the blanket and stood by the tree with her dark hair falling over her face. I was a little scared of her. She never spoke, she just swam. Out in the water, her brother Derek floated on a tire tube, his back to the shore and sunglasses on. There were pine needles sticking to the blanket, and Lisle picked them off with brown fingers while Ariadne ran down to the dock to call to Derek. He was thirteen; he stuck his hockey stick through my skate blade while we were skating the winter before and made me fall down. It was dark and cool under the pine trees, there wasn't any noise, and I wanted to go home.

Ariadne Keller came back up the path with Michael Rowe on her hip and made him wave goodbye to Lisle. She had all the pine needles cleaned off the blanket, and she walked behind us back to the house. My mother said she was shy and very intelligent, and my mother wanted me to be friends with her—it wasn't my fault that she didn't talk. She was a very good swimmer.

In the car, Ardith was listening to the radio again. Michael was put in the back seat, and he lay down and went to sleep right away, before we had even driven away from the house. He curled in on himself like a fiddlehead fern. He was cleaner than the last time, but he still had a cast of brown over him, a cloudy bloom.

We drove for nearly an hour. One or the other of them would occasionally point out pleasant vistas, but I was glad when Ardith pulled the car off on a side road and stopped at the edge of a short cliff. Over the rise of the cliff we could see the sea.

Michael was still asleep, and they decided to leave him in the car with all the doors locked and only one little window open slightly for air. Then we climbed down to the shore and the two sisters took their shoes off and walked barefoot in the crumbly sand. When we got down to the water-line where the sand was wet and firm I took my shoes off too and walked behind them in the double line of their footprints. They made long, delicate feet in the sand, wavering toward the surf and away again. Long toes and a thin edge, and then a narrow heel. I was watching their prints rather than them, going slowly, and when I looked up they were far ahead of me, walking close together, their bodies bending toward and away from each other. They seemed to have matching magnets within their breasts that pulled them together or shot them off from each other, never at peace.

The noise of the water swelling up and subsiding and the screeching of gulls blurred their voices. Sometimes part of a word would be caught by the moving air and carried back to me. They were standing still now, close, as if they had their poles correctly balanced for a moment. If I thought about them I was frightened by them, so I just looked instead of thinking.

"Catch up, Laura," Ardith called, twisting back to me. Ariadne bent to pick up a shell and they walked on, separated, the path of their feet a great Y yawning larger.

When she thought we had gone far enough, Ardith looped back and waved at Ariadne walking in the curling lip of the sea, foam to her ankles.

"Race you to the car," Ardith cried.

It was not a fair race, Ariadne was farther out, but she lifted her head and they both ran like horses. I was up on the dunes and I took a shortcut overland to get there before them to watch the finish. Ardith ran easily, in rhythm, not putting herself to too much trouble, stride falling into stride. She was way ahead by the time they were in sight around the curve of the bay, and Ariadne was already bending forward too much, trying too hard.

I heard a little noise behind me—Michael Rowe was standing up in the back seat, leaning against the car window. He couldn't get it open, and the doors were locked, so I couldn't let him out. He pressed his cheek on the window, it must have been cool. You could see how hot he was inside that car, his hair was stuck to his head, damp and curling. I stuck my nose against the glass to make him laugh, but he only moved away from the window and shut his eyes.

Down on the sand Ardith was coming into the home stretch and Ariadne was closer, running as if a fire followed her. Abruptly, Ardith stopped and looked back, and called sweetly, "You will never, ever, ever, catch me, and you know it."

Ariadne fell down on her knees, but was up again in a jerk and running again.

Ardith hit the car with her ring hand, it made a little mocking ting! loud enough for Ariadne to hear as she stumbled up the dune.

"I got him first," Ardith said.

"But it's my car." Her voice was harsh and thick.

"But I have the keys."

I really hated her then. I wasn't crazy about either of them. Michael was locked in the car still. I walked around the car away from them and waited by the back door, and after a minute Ariadne snatched the keys out of Ardith's hand and unlocked the front door.

"I have all of my body," she said in a fury—and as soon as she'd said it she laughed once, ha! as if someone had punched her in the stomach, and then looked sick. Ardith took the door handle from her gently, smiled at her and opened it. She reached in and unlocked the back door, and she held out her arms for Michael. He walked over the seat to the opposite window, where I was, but not looking at me, and leaned against the seat in the corner.

Ariadne laughed again, and Ardith suddenly lunged into the car and grabbed Michael out by the back of his shirt, and shook him—it was so quick and neat that for a second it didn't look mean, but it was, because he didn't want to go to her.

He stiffened, and Ariadne put out her arms to him, but he wouldn't look at her either. I wished so badly that I wasn't there that my head hurt, and my chest, but I crouched down lower so I could look through the car to see what they were doing. Ardith held him out stiffly away from her, half-way between them, and if they spoke, it was so quietly that I couldn't hear. But after a little time she bent down and put Michael back in the back seat, and leaned farther forward and unlocked it for me. Then she walked around to the passenger side, and Ariadne (who was still standing by the door, watching her) waited until Ardith was inside the car before getting in herself.

She drove.

After about ten miles Ariadne suddenly spoke; no-one had talked till then. "Ardith couldn't have children, Laura, that's why she gets angry." Ardith had her pointed face turned to watch her sister, but Ariadne only looked at the road, and glanced up fiercely to catch Michael in the rear-view mirror.

"I can't believe you're saying the things you're saying," Ardith said.

"She needs to have her cake and eat it and have it and eat it and have it, and a picture of it, and a recipe for it, and the *candles* always burning but never burning down..."

"Everything, I need to have everything, that's the thing, Laura, and I think she's right. I'd like to have Michael now. Michael, climb over the top, sweetheart—come and sit on my knee, baby."

He did try, I was shocked. He scrambled up and leaned on the front seat and tried to pull himself over, and Ardith pulled under his arms, but at the same time Ariadne was stopping the car, making the brakes hiss but not squeal, and I was yanking on the waist of his pants to keep him in the back.

Ariadne got out of the car like a snake, like a fuse, and opened Ardith's door as fast as light. She held it and waited, and Ardith got out, and they walked behind the car and talked to each other in low voices for a while. Michael and I sat still. He wouldn't talk—I hadn't ever heard him talk.

After a while they came back into the car and Ariadne drove off again, and nobody spoke at all. Ardith sat beside her in the front and did her lipstick and flipped through her bag and rustled generally all the way home.

Michael and I sat in the back with the windows open a crack. He looked awful, but he didn't want his hand held or anything. They dropped me at my own house without coming in.

"Laura, this has been a bad treat," Ariadne said when she stopped the car. "Wait a second. Thank you very much for jumping off the roof to your peril—take this and be better sisters than we are." She gave me a $5 bill.

I stood on the grass until they had driven away and I was just going to go in when Cecy came around the corner of the house crying.

"Somebody stole the scooter," she said, forgetting to be mad at me.

"I'm not going to fight with you any more," I told her.

"Okay," she said. "Or Sam?"

"I never fight with him anyway, he won't fight."

"Do you mean it?"

"If I start, you tell me."

We went inside and down into the hidey-hole under the porch stairs where we kept the flashlight, but we used a candle instead to save the batteries. It was a fancy candle, beeswax with a willow pattern in blue wax wrapped around it by some amazing process, which we had broken by mistake and then hidden in the hide before a dinner party. The smell was particularly good in the narrow angles of the hide, and the yellowy light was comforting to me.

"We'd better get Sam to tell you if you start," Cecy said.

"Okay. And I'm not going to lie any more."

Sam came in with three peaches that he said Mommy had said he should bring and eat with us, really ripe ones just washed so some of the fuzz was smoothed off.

"Daddy had to go to a confession," Sam said.

"I remember when he went to one when we were in Manitoba and I thought it was a confession from a crook, remember? And you told me it was an axe murderer?" Cecy knocked me on my arm for a pat, not hitting me.

"I thought it was an axe murderer. Something he said, he said something about it that made me thing it was so terrible..."

"It was a man who had hurt his wife," Sam said. "He'd hurt her really badly, stabbed her with a knife when they were fighting, you were right."

"I don't know how he knows all this stuff," I said to Cecy.

"He gets told. And then we tell him things too, and he puts them together."

"This time, I am telling you to take my peach pit upstairs and Cecy's too and bring us something to read and steal another candle."

"Okay," he said, and he went.

"Something terrible is going to happen," I said to Cecy.

We never found the scooter, it was a bad day.

Cecy and I were on the no-window side in the afternoon eating Vachon cakes with caramel in them from my \$5, and it was the last cakes of the five dollars, so it must have been at least two weeks since the drive. Sam was running round and round the house ten times so we would each give him a bite, and we were laughing at his knees going by each time pump pump, which we could see from between the yellow flicks of the forsythia. In between passes we leaned our heads back on each other's shoulders and let the caramel run out of the tops of the cakes onto our tongues and chins, and we had our shoes off so that the sandy dirt would force up between our toes.

Before Sam had gone round seven times my mother came out of the house with the baby in the basket and called for us— we could see the basket dangling from her arm, so we only waited till she rounded the corner to the back, and scrambled out to follow her. I gave Cecy my cake to hold; she didn't want to because the chocolate had melted partly from holding it, but I shoved it at her and ran.

"Laura!" my mother was calling. She had put the basket on the low table and she was peeling back the blanket just enough to give the baby air. "Get your shoes, Laura, I need you to come with me quickly—where is Cecy?—Cecy, we'll be back as soon as we can.... I've left a message for Daddy and he'll come home as soon as he gets it, so don't worry."

Cecy was trying to hide the Vachon cakes behind her back and listen both at the same time, but she didn't need to bother, because my mother wasn't looking at her anyway, she was searching for her glasses in her summer purse.

"Laura, quickly, I said! Run and get your shoes, I'll be in the car."

"Where are you going?" Cecy whispered.

I tried to look mysterious, but she knew I didn't know, so I ran to get my shoes from the forsythia and she stayed by the baby's basket looking lonely, with the Vachon cakes oozing out of her hands.

In the car my mother said, "I need you to come with me because I don't know what is happening exactly, and I may need you to help with the children. If I can, I'll leave you in the car, but if I call you you'll have to come immediately, and keep calm and be helpful and quiet."

"Where are we going?"

"To the Kellers' house."

"What's the matter?"

"I don't know yet, Lisle phoned to say please come."

"But what do you think?"

"Laura, don't talk now. What I think is that something terrible has happened, and you will stay in the car till I find out."

It didn't seem like a very long ride to Ariadne Keller's house this time. But it was quiet, and heavy, and the air was different out under the sky than it had been under the forsythia. When my mother parked the car and walked down the steps I tried the old trick of smiling to make the sun come out, which if you do slowly enough can sometimes happen, but it didn't work. The whole street, all Whitlock Edge, was still. No doors banged and no-one rode by on their bikes—you could hear the water lapping at the dock. I was Lisle open the front door, but it was so far away and so hidden by leaves that I couldn't see what was wrong. My mother took her shoulder and went inside with her.

I was getting scared out in the car. The windows were all down and the seats smelled because it was so hot, and I didn't want to sit there anymore. I didn't want to go into the house either, because I suddenly started to think about the axe murderer who Daddy had heard the confession from, and how all the noise in their house must have stopped after he was finished. But that wasn't real, I remembered that we had made that up.

My legs were stuck to the seat, and when I moved them they stuck again. Then I heard a door banging finally, but it was the Kellers' back door, the screen, and I couldn't stand it any longer, so I thought I would run down to the lake to see if some of the children were there and they might know what was the matter.

I pushed the car door shut carefully and quietly so my mother wouldn't hear me leaving, and I skimmed around the side of the house running low so she wouldn't see me through the windows—I was going so fast I didn't stop till I got to the pine path though the trees, but then I did stop.

I couldn't understand what it was for a minute, they were all standing around a lump. Lisle and her brother Derek and two of the littler children and my mother, only my mother was bending down. I didn't dare go any nearer, but my eyes refocused like a telescope and the awful shape resolved itself into something I knew. It was Ariadne Keller with her hair unbound lying on the pebble shore with the boy Michael in her arms, and I thought they were both dead, they were so drowned wet. Not wet and shining like you would be after swimming on a hot heavy day, but just drenched like from rain, their bodies left on the shore in all their clothes, slimy and dark from the wet. Her hair was black and fell all around her face and neck, and some of it fell on Michael too. My mother rose up with Michael in her arms, or tried to, but Ariadne's arms came up too, and all the other children moved away a little in slow fright. My mother said something low, and then she looked up and saw me standing there, and she said, "Come down, Laura, I need you."

There were still no other people there, and Lisle and Derek couldn't do it, but all by herself it would have been awkward to remove Ariadne's arms from the boy, it would have made it worse for the others. So I went down to the mound on the shore and Lisle and Derek parted away. My feet moved by themselves in a prim trot, sure and light on the needles, and I didn't need to be told what to do. I took one hand of Ariadne Keller at a time and pried the fingers open—it was not too hard. I kept my back in between the fingers and Lisle and Derek, and my mother was looking at the smaller girls to calm them.

Her fingers were cool and a little flabby without her excited grasping appetite inside them—but she wasn't dead, she was just unconscious. I never thought she was dead, dead people are supposed to look happy. I laid her fingers down on her stomach, and one of her hands fell away upwards and grazed her breast, and someone winced. It sounds so slow, but really it was all done quickly, as if my mother had changed the way time went so that nothing would be jerky or frightening for the children.

She was already turning away with Michael, moving swiftly away up to the verandah, and she looked over her shoulder to me.

"Chafe her hands and cheeks, Laura, try to keep her warm. Derek will bring down a blanket in a minute. She will be all right, Lisle. You can watch Michael with me until help comes now...."

Lisle was still standing where she had been, staring down at her mother, and she looked so desperate that I started to cry for a second but I stopped it in time before it got up into my face.

"She went into the water because he was drowning," she said, and she walked up after my mother. She glanced at Derek as she went by and made him go with her. The two little girls stayed down with me—I could never remember their names.

It was pretty calm under the trees with everybody gone to the house except me and the little girls and Ariadne Keller who looked now like she was sleeping, less dead. I kept rubbing her hands between mine, and we all kept our eyes on them. There was sand in patterns on her arms, like the baby game where you draw your name in spit on your skin and then shake sand on it. Way way in the distance we could all hear a siren, and it surprised me, I thought maybe this was all going to be quiet, that my mother had fixed it so no-one would know something awful had happened.

"Will they lock her up and throw away the key?" one of the little girls asked, the one who didn't have her three fingers stuck in her mouth.

"Why?" I asked her.

"That's what she said, that's what she says all the time. Because she walked into the water with him."

The other one took her fingers out of her mouth. "I think Lisle should have left her in the water."

It was quiet for a minute. She still had her shoes on, sandals with thin straps. I tried to decide what colour they had been before they got dark with wet.

"She walked right in there with him," a voice came out of a bush behind the girls—the younger boy who had been hiding there came out walking like a frog to have a look now that my mother was gone. "Right into the lake, right in...." They all nodded, not looking at each other, just looking at her.

They were really scary, they made me want to throw up, but instead I kept looking at Ariadne Keller's hands, all long and pale brown now, and the children didn't say anything more. She had never looked like she had any children at all, and they didn't look like they had any mother at all.

The siren got louder and louder and then cut out at the turn-off from St. Margaret's Bay Road—even though it was so far the sound was clear in the silence. We heard them drive up, and the crunch of the red clay bits in the far driveway, and then we heard doors shutting and opening and people moving, and the front door, and my mother's voice, and all this time, hearing all these important moving things going on and about to happen, we just sat on the shore with Ariadne not stirring, still. I got worried suddenly that they would forget about us, about me, and I would have to stay there with those scary kids until dark and then they would probably eat me or get out their axes.

My mother came to the top of the path and called the little girls by name, I don't know how she remembered them. They

ran away up the path and past her, and out through the trees
to some hide of their own. She wavered as if she might follow
them, but she came down instead, with the ambulance men
following her. She was still holding Michael in her arms, and
he lolled over the edges like Cecy had drooped over Ariadne
Keller's arms on the spaghetti night. Nothing on him was
broken, but now that he'd been out of the water for a while you
could see where the blood was coming from that had washed
over him before. One split on his forehead was leaking blood
down over his eye, still pinkish and weak over his pinchy face,
and there were dark bruises on his skin now purpling round
the edges.

Lisle had followed the men down, and she saw one of them
staring at Michael in my mother's arms.

"She went into the water because he was drowning," she
told them. "She went into the lake to save him, he was rolling
on the log and getting hurt so she went out to get him," she
said, and then she turned right straight around and threw up
in the bushes.

I was all right until the ambulance men told me to let go a
little rudely, and one of them pulled my arm, and I hit him
really hard as I got up, and then I had to say, "I'm very sorry,"
because I hadn't meant to hit him at all, and I was amazed that
I had done it and also very ashamed. But my mother was there
and she had given Michael away to one of the men, and she
held on to me and said I could wait in the car, and that Lisle
was there already and she would be glad if I would help her and
Derek, so then I had to move away from Ariadne Keller, lying
on the shore.

I was fine when we went home, and I was fine later on, and I
was fine when my father took me into his study to tell me what
had really happened and to say that Ariadne Keller was very
unhappy and had wanted for a little while to die, and that she
would be going to a sanatorium, which I knew was the loony-
bin. And the whole time he was talking to me and trying to

explain how it could have happened without frightening me, I wasn't frightened. There was no need to be frightened. I was just miserable.

I had a nightmare in the middle of the night, I think because of hitting the ambulance man by mistake. I dreamed that I was beating up somebody. I'd gotten in a really bad temper and I just started beating up people. It was a backwards dream—I could have dreamed that I was beating up someone and woken up to find I was punching my pillow, but in this dream I began at the pillow, which made me terrified to wake up, because I thought if I've been dreaming that I'm beating up a pillow, when I wake up I will really be beating up a person, who will I be beating? Then the pillow I was holding became a child, and I thought, I can't beat this child, I can't be doing this—so I know what I'll do, it's not happening, I'll take us under the water. I'll go under the water and it will not happen. You can't beat somebody up under the water, and the water will comfort him.

But under the water it was so awful, it was so thick. I couldn't move quickly, I couldn't get my long brown thin legs to move, or my long arms to untwine from around Michael Rowe. If I'd thought to go into the ocean it would have worked. But the ocean was far away, and the lake was right there.

Cecy woke me up, I was curled right down at the bottom of the bed, and weeping. She sat on my bed with me for ages and I told her about the dream, and she played with my hair until I stopped crying.

"Do you know what?" I said to her. "I love you to pieces."

"Yes, and I love you back together again," she said.

The ambulance men had pulled a stretcher down the path and they were going to put her on it. She looked so sad even with her eyes closed that I thought she might be pretending. She might just be wanting someone to carry her, like she had said to me a long time before.